Libby Gleeson is an acclaimed and much-loved author of over 30 books for children and teenagers. Her books have been shortlisted for Children's Book Council awards eleven times and she has won three times – most recently the Early Childhood Award for *Amy and Louis*, illustrated by Freya Blackwood. *The Great Bear* (with Armin Greder) was the first Australian title to win the prestigious Bologna Ragazzi Award, in 2000.

Libby has been a teacher and lecturer and a speaker at national conferences, and is actively involved in writers' organisations. In 1997 she was awarded the Lady Cutler Award for Services to Children's Literature and in 2007 she was made Member of the Order of Australia (AM) for services to literature and literacy education.

You can find Libby's website at
www.libbygleeson.com.au

Other books by Libby Gleeson

Novels

Eleanor, Elizabeth

I Am Susannah

Dodger

Love Me, Love Me Not

Refuge

The Queen of the Universe

The Hannah series

Skating on Sand

Hannah Plus One

Hannah and the Tomorrow Room

Picture books

Big Dog

Where's Mum?

Mum Goes to Work

Sleeptime

Shutting the Chooks In

Cuddletime

Amy and Louis

and with Armin Greder

Uncle David

The Princess and the Perfect Dish

The Great Bear

(winner, Bologna Ragazzi Award)

An Ordinary Day

Mahtab's Story

Libby Gleeson

ALLEN&UNWIN

Thanks to the Bundanon Trust
for periods of unfettered writing time

First published in 2008

Allen & Unwin
83 Alexander St
Crows Nest NSW 2065
Australia
Phone: (61 2) 8425 0100
Fax: (61 2) 9906 2218
Email: info@allenandunwin.com
Web: www.allenandunwin.com

National Library of Australia
Cataloguing-in-Publication entry:

Gleeson, Libby, 1950– .
  Mahtab's story.

  ISBN 9781741753349 (pbk.).

  I. Title.

  A823.3

Text and cover design by Sandra Nobes
Typeset by Tou-Can Design
Printed by McPherson's Printing Group, Australia

10 9 8 7 6 5

Teachers notes available at www.allenandunwin.com/teachersnotes

For Nahid and Dorothy

Chapter One

MAHTAB ACHED.

She rubbed her freezing hands together and pressed them into her mouth, sucking the life back into them. Kilometre after kilometre, the cold continued. Icy air seeped up from the floor of the truck and made its way through the layers of her cotton weave trousers. It slipped through the timber joins near her head and chilled her face, her neck and her shoulders. It brought with it a fine, pale powder that worked its way into her hair, her eyes and her nose. All she could taste was diesel and dust.

Mahtab wanted to leap up, to drum her heels against the floor, to fling her arms into the air and

1

yell as if her heart and lungs would burst. But her throat was a closed and choking trapdoor. She was compelled and sentenced to silence.

Farhad crouched beside her, his head not quite to her shoulder, exhausted and dulled into sleep. In the shadows, Mahtab could just make out the shape of her mother beside him. Soraya, thumb in mouth, was pressed against her, each as still as a block of stone.

Every rock, every pothole and gouge in the road jarred her body against the rough timber that held her in.

Would they ever get there? Would it ever be over?

~~~

When had the fog of darkness and fear wrapped itself around the house? That fog that closed them in, all except Grandfather, Uncle Wahid and her own father too, until... She pushed that thought away. Think of before. Think of times like the wedding of Aunt Mina and Uncle Wahid when she was six. No fog then. They had all gone out to the hall and there was music and dancing and rows of tables laden with dishes of goat and lamb kebab, sweet fruit and yoghurt. Aunt Mina was queen for the night and even Mahtab had henna on her hands and had stayed up long after Farhad and the baby Soraya fell asleep. But Soraya wasn't a baby any more. She was almost ready to learn to read.

The fog must have been there the afternoon with the kites or why would Uncle Wahid have come running? 'Stop! STOP!' he yelled and the sleeves of his shirt flew wide and the afternoon sun glinted off the red lights of his beard. Farhad and Reza were racing around the yard with their kites. They challenged each other, laughing and whipping the strings, sharp with their fragments of glass, to slide against each other. It was a weird dance. They risked one cutting the other free, sending the bright blue and red squares flying, high into the open sky, across the city, lost for ever.

Mahtab and Leila sat under the lemon tree and watched.

'You must never,' screamed Uncle Wahid, 'never play this way again.' He grabbed the strings, hauling them to his chest so swiftly that his hands were torn by the shiny splinters and his blood splashed first on the pale cotton of his trousers and then on the grass at his feet. 'You are putting the whole family in danger, you will be killed and your fathers and your mothers and your brothers and your sisters and your cousins and what do you think you are doing? You have been told that everything has changed and you are never, never, never to play like this again.'

Everything had changed. Mahtab held tightly to Leila's hand. They watched as the boys, snivelling and shrunken, took the shovel and dug a hole under the lemon tree and buried the folded kites in the hard brown earth. They kicked dirt on the brightly coloured fabric, and when they had trodden the clods down Uncle put his arms around their shoulders and patted them, guiding them back into the house. They lay, curled up like babies, crying on their beds.

～～～

Around that time, Leila began to come less often. Before, when their parents sat downstairs, talking and feasting on plates piled high with apricots and almonds, pears and pistachios, Mahtab and she slept above them on the roof. Warm under a single summer blanket, they planned their lives. 'I will be a teacher like my Aunt Mariam,' said Leila. 'And I will have five children and a handsome husband.'

'I will be a doctor like Grandma's sister,' said Mahtab. 'And my husband will be handsome too. I think I'll have three children, all girls because boys are so much trouble.' They giggled and pointed at the sky and claimed the stars as their own.

～～～

But then school had stopped. For a time secret lessons continued with a tutor, but then Leila and her family were gone.

～～～

'Where is she?' said Mahtab. 'Why didn't she say goodbye? She is my friend, my sister.'

'They are gone to Iran,' her father said. 'They left secretly because there was great danger for her family. Her father knew that if he stayed...' He turned away.

'Will I see her again?' Mahtab seized his hand and looked up at him. He did not meet her gaze but pulled her tightly towards him and kissed the top of her head.

'Who knows, my Mahtab? Who knows?'

Mahtab lay on her bed, awake long into the night. Why was Leila's family in danger? Were they now safe from whatever that danger had been? Was she somewhere in Iran and was she thinking of Mahtab? Were she, Mahtab, and her family in danger also? Would they too go to Iran?

~~~

The house was different. She remembered nights when the whole family sat around the low table. They warmed their feet by the coal brazier under the blanket. Her grandmother poured tea and passed around the steaming glasses. The gold chains and coins at her wrist jangled, flicking the soft light from the kerosene lamp into the faces of Mahtab, Farhad, Soraya and their cousins Reza and baby Rasheed.

Her grandfather told stories: The Thousand and One Nights, Aladdin, Ali Baba, Sinbad, The Ebony Horse. The younger ones fell asleep but Mahtab willed her eyes to stay open as he stroked his beard and his gentle voice spun the tales and more tea was brewed. Finally her eyelids drooped and she rested her head in her grandmother's lap.

~~~

Now that fog had seeped into the house and into their lives. There would be no education for girls. Mahtab could no longer go to school. Her mother no longer went to work. The women almost never left the house. Instead they sat at home and waited till Mahtab's father, her uncle and her grandfather came home at the end of the day. They brought with them news of the outside, fearful news, which they shared with the women in hushed voices. Mahtab was sent from the room.

~~~

She listened. She hushed Farhad and Soraya as they chased each other from the kitchen to the storeroom and back again. She stood in the doorway and heard the words 'men in black turbans... whips... beatings... the knock on the door in the middle of the night... hanging... shooting... public stoning... Taliban.' On one evening her grandmother found her there, her ear pressed to the door.

'Go to your room this minute,' she said in a voice that Mahtab had not heard before. Later that night she came and lay on the bed beside Mahtab and stroked her hair. 'I am so sorry to speak harshly,' she said, 'so sorry and you all so young.'

'Will someone come and knock on our door?' Mahtab's voice was only a whisper.

Her grandmother didn't answer but pulled her close and held her so tightly that Mahtab fell asleep to the rhythm of the old woman's beating heart.

~~~~~

Then, one night, her father and grandfather did not come home at the usual time. Mahtab sat quietly in the shadows, listening as her mother, aunt and grandmother paced the floor, speaking in urgent whispers. Uncle Wahid went to search. The whole house waited. Some time in the darkness her father was there, alive, his face black with bruising, one eye closed and swollen, broad stripes of blood seeping through the cotton shirt on his back. Of Grandfather, there was nothing: no body, no word.

~~~~~

Night after night the whispering and the weeping continued.

~~~~~

Mahtab sat in the dark outside her parents' bedroom door, watching over her father. As long as she stayed within sight she knew he would get better. She watched her mother tending the bruises on his face, the cuts on his chest, the slashes across his back from the whips. When he moved, slowly, into the sitting room, Mahtab followed. When he rested in the garden, in the sun, she sat at his feet. She brought him his favourite slices of apple, poured him his tea with sprigs of mint. He said little but stared at her and at Farhad and Soraya as they played on the swing and splashed in the paddling pool.

One night she woke to hear sounds from her parents' room. Uncle Wahid's voice and then Aunt Mina: 'How can you leave?' She was weeping. 'Our family has lived in this city forever. You were born here. Your children were born here. All of the family is buried here. You will be strangers in a strange land. You will be leaving everything you know and love behind.'

'We know that.' This was her mother's voice. 'But I do not want my young children to be buried before their time or to have to bury me while they are young. I want them free from fear, free of all this. We must go, for them.' Mahtab knew she had been crying too.

'But it is too dangerous to leave.'

'It is too dangerous to stay.'

'It means a long drive over the mountains, and even before then they have their men everywhere. And bandits too, who will take your money. There are even wild animals, wolves. You can trust nobody.'

'We can trust nobody in this place either,' Mahtab's father said. 'Who knows if they will come for me again? Look what they did to our father. Our neighbour's son has been taken. In every street someone has gone.'

'Please don't go. Please.'

'We've made up our minds. We must go.'

~~~

Gradually her father's body healed but he no longer went to work in the daytime and at night the books Mahtab so loved to hear him read stayed unopened. He never sat at the low table and taught her the way to move her chess pieces to outwit him, and all stories, all laughter, all joking seemed to have gone from him.

Then one night he came and sat on her bed. 'I need to talk to you,' he said. 'Your mother and I have made a very big decision.'

'Are we going to Iran?'

He shook his head. 'We are leaving, but not for Iran. First I want to tell you a story.' He folded his arms and took a deep breath. 'When I was a young man at the University, I met a stranger in a coffee shop. He was about my age and he came from a faraway land called Australia. He was travelling from his country to Europe on a great adventure, and he had stopped here because many, many years ago, his great-great-great-grandfather had left Afghanistan and crossed the seas to Australia to work with camels. So this

9

young man wanted to be in the land of his ancestors. I brought him home and he stayed with us for some time. He wanted to learn as much about our country as he could and so we talked long into the evenings. In return he told us much about his country. I am going to tell you everything I can remember because I want you to know that the way we are living here, now, is not the only way. One day, like that man's great-great-great-grandfather, we may have to leave.'

'You mean,' Mahtab hesitated, 'go to his country, his Australia?'

Her father nodded.

'But would we come back?'

'I don't know. God willing. Listen well and remember. If we go to that man's country, you would not stay at home. You would go to school and you could dream again of being a doctor like your great-aunt or a teacher or whatever you wanted to be. The women work as they did here, before. You and Mum could walk in the sunshine with your faces bare and there are no men in black turbans who can take you and beat you because they do not like the way you dress or what you believe or what you say. There, whips are for horses and camels.'

'Is it a long way?'

He nodded.

'Can I take all my things?'

'Maybe not everything. It is further than Iran. Tomorrow, I will show you in the atlas.'

~~~~~

It was still dark when Mahtab woke. She lay still. Australia. She said the word over and over but she had no picture in her mind. What would it look like? How would they get there? She crept towards her parents' room. She paused in the doorway, listening to the soft murmuring of their voices. Again her mother was crying and she heard her saying, 'We will die out there. In the mountains. On the sea. It is not too late to choose Iran.'

Mahtab clutched the front of her nightdress. Her body trembled. *Choose Iran. Leila is there. We will be together and then we will return and I do not want to journey through the mountains and over the sea. I am afraid.*

And her father. 'There is no future for us here or in Iran. We will have the life I have told you about. We will be free to live the way we choose. You must believe. There will be happiness and joy for us when we arrive there. I promise you.'

Mahtab tiptoed away. Happiness and joy. Farhad and Soraya, in their room, were sleeping. She watched their bodies shifting slightly with each breath. Did they know? Had her father told them? She felt her way to her room in the darkness and took down from her bookshelf the rag doll her grandmother had made for her. How long since she had fallen asleep with it beside her on the pillow? She burrowed deep into the mattress, wrapping her arms tightly around the doll, rubbing her cheek against the soft fabric. She pulled the blanket up over her head. It made a dark secret space that no one, nothing could enter.

Chapter Two

COLD, SO COLD.

Mahtab sat on the hard wooden floor of the truck. She was wedged in by furniture, boxes and sacks, her knees caught up under her chin. How long had they been travelling like this? Two hours? Four hours? Six?

~~~

It had been night time when they left. Her father shook her awake. 'Mahtab, Mahtab. Get up. We're leaving.'

'What? Where?' She sat up.

'There is a truck outside. We are leaving for Pakistan.'

'Pakistan? All of us?' She leant against him as she pushed aside her blankets and pressed her feet into the soft wool of the carpet.

He shook his head. 'Just us. You, me, Mum, Farhad and Soraya.'

'But Grandma...?'

'Uncle Wahid will look after her. She says she is too old. Get dressed, quickly.'

At the end of the bed were her clothes – two pairs of trousers, a long-sleeved shirt, two jackets, gloves, her warmest boots.

'Put them all on. It's cold where we're going. You'll need them all. And you can't bring anything extra.'

She started to pull on her clothes. Why couldn't she bring her doll, the special book of poems that Grandpa had made, her favourite photos, an extra scarf? He was already gone.

The photo of Leila stared at her from its silver frame. She slipped the photo out and pushed it down into her pocket. She stumbled to the front door like an overdressed clown. Soraya was dozing in their mother's arms and Farhad was beside her, stamping his feet and blowing his warm breath onto his gloved hands. Two suitcases and bags of food leant against the wall.

'Listen carefully.' Her father shook Soraya awake and knelt her on the floor with Farhad and Mahtab.

He looked directly from one to another. 'You are going to hide in a special part of the truck with Mum. Try to sleep. Sometimes we might stop and you can come out and have a run around to stretch your legs. But, and this is so important, if I bang twice on the wall of the cabin, we are coming to a special checkpoint and you must make no sound. None. Not even a whisper. You understand? If they find you, we are all dead.'

Farhad and Soraya nodded, wide-eyed. Mahtab too. Suddenly she was more awake than ever in her life before. Dead. Her body stiffened. She would not let her breath make a sound as it left her body.

'My brave, brave children.' His hand was shaking as he pushed her hair back from her face and pressed his lips against her forehead.

They crept outside.

Mahtab could just make out the shape of the truck. Beneath a loose tarpaulin were what looked like a table and three wardrobes lashed onto the back with a stack of smaller furniture: chairs, blanket boxes and cabinets. Then there were sacks stuffed full and still more boxes. A man appeared, silent, out of the darkness. He lifted down a heavy sack of grain, held back the tarpaulin and pushed aside a wardrobe. A narrow corridor was revealed between two of the cabinets. Mahtab's mother climbed up, squeezed into the space and disappeared. Farhad and Soraya were lifted up and Mahtab followed, feeling her way forward. It smelt damp and musty and led to an opening not much bigger than a tabletop. Their bodies bumped and brushed against each other as they settled into sitting positions. The wardrobe was pushed back into place and the tarpaulin dropped down. Their father and the outside world were gone.

Her mother pulled all three of them close. *'God, send your prayers and mercy to the prophet Mohammed and all his followers.'* She kept her arms wrapped around the children as the truck moved forward slowly. Mahtab pressed her eyes tightly closed.

~~~~

Now she knew why her grandmother had come into the bedroom the night before and sat watching her as she fell asleep, why Grandma bent and kissed her and then returned and did it again. When Mahtab opened her eyes, her grandmother took from her own wrist the bracelet of gold coins, linked with gold chain, and clasped it on Mahtab's wrist. 'So you will always remember,' she said, and she slipped away.

Where were they driving? Down to the end of the street. She knew that part of the road. Then they turned to the right. That meant they were going past the bazaar and the shops where she used to go with Mum to buy the fruit and vegetables. When they could go out. So long ago now. Were people arriving, spreading out the trestles covered in golden apples, sweet yellow melons, grapes and mulberries? Then there was the open space and the Friday mosque with its tiles of sky-blue, its patterns of other blues and greens in bands broken by lines of gold. She tried to remember what came next.

She listened for signs that the day had started. Were there other trucks or carts around? Were people walking along the side of the road? She heard the squelching of tyres on gravel, the groaning of gears, and felt the thud of the truck's wheel dropping into a pothole. Nothing more.

～～

Mahtab shifted position and her shoulder struck the corner of a table but she made no sound. She felt her mother's hand gently rubbing on the spot where it hurt.

'Are you all right?' her mother whispered.

'Why didn't we say goodbye to Grandma?'

'She'll understand.'

Farhad and Soraya were quiet beside her. They seemed to sleep but in the dark Mahtab couldn't tell.

Gradually, faint slivers of light seeped through the walls of the truck. Above Mahtab's head were planks of wood and on them were more sacks of grain. What if a bandit with a gun or a checkpoint Talib wanted them taken off and the furniture moved?

What if they wanted to know what lay beneath? Her stomach muscles shivered. Her belly was a stone of ice, solid. Cold breath forced its way through her throat, her nose, her mouth.

'Most of all they want money,' Dad had said.

But what if he was wrong?

'Can we talk?' Farhad stirred.

'Yes,' said his mother, 'but just quietly. This truck is so noisy that I don't think anyone will hear us.'

Mahtab sat silent while Farhad began, 'Will the men in black turbans get us in the mountains?'

'No.'

'Will they be in Pakistan?'

'No.'

'Will we ever see them again?'

'No. Where we are going, we hope that there will be nothing nasty or bad that can ever happen to anyone again.' Mum's hand rested in his hair.

Nothing bad or nasty. No weeping and crying in the houses because someone has been taken by the bands of Taliban carrying guns and whips? No fear that the knock on the door will bring pain and grieving? No whispered conversations that were not meant for children: conversations of beatings and shootings, of disappearing, of hangings and stonings?

Mahtab shivered. She tried to stretch. Her back ached and her neck was sore. Grandma would be awake now. Mahtab saw her walking slowly room to room then eating her breakfast with Uncle Wahid, Reza and Rasheed. Aunt Mina would be there too. The usual start to the day. Were they wondering where the truck was now? Did they know where exactly the truck was going? In fact, where was the truck going? Mahtab tried to remember the maps she had seen. She knew there were fields and open space around the edge of the town – flat, fertile country, orchards and wheat-fields, easy to drive through. But soon there would be mountains. Huge mountains stretched almost the length of the country. She had never seen them but she knew from the atlas that Pakistan was on the other side. A long, long way on the other side.

Soraya pushed her head against Mahtab's knee. 'How long will we be in here?'

'I don't know,' said Mahtab. 'A long time. Go to sleep.'

'I don't want to.'

'Go to sleep.'

'You can't make me.'

'There's nothing else to do.'

Soraya grew quiet then but Mahtab couldn't sleep. Her mind played over and over the conversations of the past few days. Uncle Wahid at first saying that they must not go and then changing his mind and saying it was the right thing to do. Aunt Mina, shaking her head and fighting to hold back tears. Grandma urging them on. And then there were her mother's tears at night when she thought no one was listening and her father's words: happiness and joy. She repeated them now, happiness and joy, happiness and joy. In the darkness they felt strangely empty.

~~~

She must have slept because she woke to the sound of the truck slowing to a halt. Had there been two bangs on the cabin wall? What was happening?

A door slammed. Boots crunched on gravel. The truck rocked as furniture was shifted and she heard her father's voice. 'Rest time. Stretch your legs. Come out and breathe some fresh air.'

They slid out like strange burrowing creatures coming from their holes to the surface. Their legs wouldn't hold them up properly and they slumped against the body of the truck. Mahtab's eyes hurt in the early-morning light. She squinted and turned away from the glare leaping from flecks of white stone.

'We're in the foothills of the mountains,' her father said. 'Soon we start really climbing.'

'No sign of them?' Mahtab's mother shielded her eyes with her hand, gazing into the distance.

'No. Not yet.'

Mahtab knelt with her mother and father, facing south-west.

'In the Name of Allah, the Beneficent, the Merciful. Praise be to Allah, Lord of the worlds...'

The words, the rhythms were so familiar. It didn't matter that she was not on the rug at home. Surely they would be all right.

~~~~

They sat then in the shade of the truck and ate rounds of bread and kebab, dripping meat juice over their chins.

'How far is Pakistan?' Mahtab rolled the last piece of bread into a tube and bit into it.

'Maybe two weeks. We're not going by any main roads. We'll criss-cross all the back ways to avoid people.'

'So we're not going to any towns?'

Her father shook his head. 'Only when we absolutely have to. When our diesel runs low. And you will all stay hidden. We have enough food.'

Two weeks. Two weeks crouched and hiding, body rigid, waiting every minute for the two loud bangs that might come on the cabin wall. Two weeks of fear, of the ice stone in the belly, of holding your breath, of whispering, of blocking from your mind everything you know or have heard of what they can do. They. Taliban. The whip-carrying men in black turbans. The ones who had been so cruel to her father, to Grandpa...

~~~~

'I don't want to go back in there.' Soraya buried herself against her mother's legs. 'It's too dark.'

'You have to, little one.' Her mother crouched beside her and rubbed her back. 'It's the only way we can get to Pakistan.'

'It's too dark,' she said again.

'Come on, Soraya.' Farhad took her hand. 'We must be like Ali Baba and this is that special cave and we have to hide in here because the forty thieves might come back. They'll never, ever find us here because it's so dark and we'll hide.'

'And we'll find the treasure.'

'Can you remember?' said Farhad.

'Gold and silver,' said Soraya. 'Lots and lots of coins and carpets and cloth of silk and brocade.'

'Open Sesame,' said Farhad, and their father held the tarpaulin back so they could all enter the dark space.

'Close Sesame,' Soraya instructed as she pushed herself back against the bulky form of her mother.

~~~~

Darkness again. Now Mahtab felt the truck climbing higher and higher. She leant back against a wardrobe.

Farhad is right, it is like a cave. It's as if we are inside the Earth except that we are bouncing along, hitting potholes and skidding along bits of the surface of the road. She then imagined the Earth doing that – bouncing through space, hitting whatever would be the equivalent of a pothole, bouncing around stars and planets – and she found herself giggling.

Her mother had begun to tell the story of Ali Baba again. She told of the poor man in the forest cutting wood for a living. He sees a great group of horsemen coming towards him and, fearful, he climbs a tree to hide. He realises that there is a huge rock nearby and the horsemen, who he decides are robbers, stop in front of this rock and their leader utters the words 'Open Sesame.' The rock rolls aside and reveals the opening of a cave. The robbers take into the cave all their bags of gold and silver coins and then they come out and go off in the direction they came from. Ali Baba waits for some time and then he decides to try and enter the cave. He utters those magic words, 'Open Sesame,' and the rock flies open and shows that there in the large cavern, lit by holes in the roof, are sacks and sacks of treasure.

'Tell me again what the treasure is,' whispered Soraya.

'Gold...'

Two loud bangs on the wall sounded between them and the cabin.

Mahtab stiffened, snatched her hand up over her mouth.

No sound. Don't make a sound.

The signal.

A checkpoint.

Taliban.

She froze.

The truck's gears ground slowly down and stopped.

She heard the doors open and she pictured her father and the driver getting out. She heard them step away from the truck. Then muffled words.

She pressed her eyes tightly closed. Farhad's hand gripped hers.

'When you are very scared,' her grandfather had said to her once, 'count backwards from a hundred. By the time you get to zero, the worrying moment may have passed.'

One hundred, ninety-nine, ninety-eight, ninety-seven, ninety-six... Had her grandfather done this when the Talib smashed through the door of his office and dragged him out? *Ninety-five, ninety-four, ninety-three*... Had he done it when he stood there and heard their accusations? *Ninety-two, ninety-one, ninety*... And had he done this when they raised their whips and struck him and then their guns and shot him dead? What number was she up to? The voices were continuing.

Were they arguing? Would the soldiers not let them through? What story was her father telling them? Would they believe him? Would they know of that time when he was taken before? Of her grandfather?

Boots clomped around the back of the truck. Stones were kicked aside. Something slapped against a tyre. A kick? A swipe from a whip?

A shadow passed in front of the narrow slit that let the sliver of sunlight through.

Mahtab held her breath.

Think of the numbers. Which was it again? *Eighty-nine, eighty-eight, eighty-seven . . .*

Soraya stirred. She stretched away from her mother and the tiny bracelet on her wrist scraped against wood. To Mahtab, it sounded as if wild horses were dragging chains across the bare ground. Her mother felt inside her robe and taking a cube of sugar, pressed it to Soraya's lips. This was the sign they'd arranged: suck quietly on the sugar and don't make a sound. She passed one each to Farhad and Mahtab. Even as she rolled the sugar around her mouth, Mahtab felt the sound of grains on her teeth was deafening. Surely they could be heard.

The truck doors slammed. The engine started. Her father's feet stomping against the floor set up a vibration that blocked the shaking of the truck.

Mahtab felt her whole body go loose. Every muscle had been tense, tight, and now it was as if the wind had suddenly died and she was a kite dropping lifeless to the ground.

Her mother squeezed her hand. 'Thank God, thank God, we are saved, this time.'

Mahtab wanted to giggle, to speak of anything, to fill the space they were in with words, any words. She looked from her mother to her little sister and brother.

Tears filled his eyes. As they streamed down his cheeks, he pressed his hand to his mouth and was silent.

~~~

After about twenty minutes the truck stopped again. This time there was no banging or warning noises from her father. He came to the side of the truck and pushed aside the tarpaulin and the furniture.

'Come on,' he said. 'Stretch-your-legs time again.' He pulled Mahtab down by her feet. 'How are you? Are you all right?'

She tried to stand but her legs wouldn't hold her. She fell against the back of the truck as her mother slid out and collapsed in a heap on the ground.

The air was fresh and cold. Mountain peaks disappeared into cloud. Patches of snow, only metres above them, lay as if carelessly tossed there by a passing traveller. Mahtab stared. One day Grandpa had taken down a book and shown her a picture like this. 'This is our country too,' he'd said. 'One day you may see it and know that not everything is in the towns or in villages. There are wild and beautiful places out there.'

The wind whipped the burqa over her mother's shoulders as she balanced, unsteady. She drank quickly from the water flask. 'How much did that checkpoint cost us?'

'A lot.' Dad frowned. Then he grinned, a sight Mahtab had not seen for a long time. 'But not everything. We have enough for the next one. Now it is time to pray.'

Chapter Three

THEY CLIMBED HIGHER and higher. One moment Mahtab was thrown back, her body resting against one of the wardrobes, Farhad and Soraya on top of her. Then the truck would level out for a few minutes and they would become upright again. Slow motion.

'It's as if we're stuck inside an elephant,' Mahtab hissed to Farhad. 'It's having trouble getting up this mountain.'

'No. It's a dinosaur,' he said. 'Plod, plod.' And he leant forward and marched his hands up and over Soraya's legs, her shoulders and her head. They stuffed their hands inside their mouths to stop their giggling. They could *walk* more quickly than this.

They lurched and swayed around bends as tight as the point of a star.

Mahtab settled back. Her stomach suddenly heaved and floated and then curled in upon itself. She sealed her lips as tightly as a judge's death warrant.

～～～

All the next night they drove in darkness. Higher and higher still. They wrapped their arms tightly around their bodies against the bitter cold. They breathed clouds of white air. The man drove and then her father drove and then the man drove again. They stopped and climbed down and stumbled behind rocks to relieve themselves, their fingers so frozen that buttons and zippers were almost impossible to undo. Then back again, closing out the stars and the still night air as their truck bumped and lurched its way over the rutted road.

Soraya and Farhad slept. Mahtab too, although she felt that every pothole and gouge in the road jerked her eyes open and reminded her of where she was: hidden in darkness, fleeing. Nothing else existed, no home, no outside world of houses and people, not even stars and the moon.

For ever, darkness.

～～～

Morning came but brought no change. Still the truck edged its way higher and higher. Mahtab had been awake for some time when they stopped and climbed down in the pale sunlight for some breakfast. She bit into a crisp golden apple brought from the tree at home, and leant back against a rock. Her mother and father sat close to each other, whispering, and they were joined by the man, the driver, Jamal.

Farhad took the paper bag that had held the fruit. He bunched it tightly and then dropped it on the road and kicked it towards the rocky ground that stretched above them. He cried out and raced after his paper ball, kicking it back to his father, who tossed it in the air and then flicked it to his son. Farhad dribbled it back to the group, laughing as his mother and father smiled. Jamal clapped and for a moment Mahtab felt the muscles in her face relax and her body lighten and she too lifted her hands and joined in.

~~~~~

For days their lives continued this way. Driving only on the minor roads, some of them little more than narrow, pot-holed paths fit only for donkeys, the truck with its strange cargo journeyed across the country.

On one occasion, Soraya pushed her face towards Mahtab and whispered, 'Farhad told me there are wolves and when I go outside they will eat me up.'

'He's teasing.' Mahtab cuddled her sister. 'Dad would never let anything bad happen to you.'

'A bad thing happened to Grandpa.'

'That was different. That was in the city.'

Was it different? Could Dad save them from danger? From wolves? From human wolves?

Other times Soraya pressed her body into their mother and whimpered. 'I'm freezing, Mumma.'

Then their mother would wrap herself around her and rock her and urge her to think warm thoughts. 'Remember sunshine coming through the branches of the lemon tree, the golden lemons and there you are, half dressed and paddling in the wading pool to get cool. You will be warm again, I promise.'

Then she would sing, softly, the La La song, which Mahtab had not heard her sing for many years.

La la la la sleep,
Because the night is long,
It's too early for you to count the stars yet,
Some people are smiling even in their dreams,
Some people have wet eyes even in their sleep,
La la la la sleep.

~~~

Three times, Mahtab heard the beating of two strikes against the wall of the cabin. At once her chest felt as if tight bands of steel were wrapped around it, being pulled ever tighter. The ice stone in her belly returned. Doors opened and slammed shut. She heard loud, demanding voices. One time the truck rocked as someone climbed on the tray and pushed the furniture and shoved the sacks of grain from their positions. She heard the slash of a knife tearing through a hessian sack and then grains of wheat pouring out onto the floor. Fine powder blew up and into every space between the furniture. Mahtab felt it in her eyes, her nose, her mouth. She wanted to sneeze, to spit, to clear her head. Feet stamped so close to her. Harsh voices cut through the air. She held her breath. *One hundred, ninety-nine, ninety-eight, ninety-seven*...

~~~

By the end of the first week, Mahtab felt she had never known another life. Had she really run through the yard, calling for Farhad in games of hide-and-seek, chasing Leila, squealing until told by Aunt Mina that girls did not make noise like that? Had she slept stretched out on a soft mattress, a cool fan blowing above her? Hour after hour, crouched, bouncing in the half-light, she listened as her mother told the stories over and over again.

'Ali Baba, Mum,' Farhad said.

'No, Aladdin and the Lamp,' said Soraya.

'Listen,' said their mother. 'This one is the tale of Furhad and Sheenree.'

And so the old stories were retold, of wood-carters, stone-cutters, camel-herders, traders and chieftains, warriors and beautiful, steadfast women.

Between the tellings, Mahtab willed herself to remember. First it was the house, the only home she had ever known. She pictured herself getting up in the morning, casting off the bed covers and stepping onto the rich red swirls of the carpet. The shelf above held books, pencils, paints and the things for study. Then the cupboard where her clothes hung. Brightest of them all was the dress Uncle Rahim had sent from Paris that was too big for her. Now she'd never wear the yellow silk, never feel it fall softly over her skin. Never sit with Leila telling each other again of their future selves, faces made up, jewellery on, waiting for their husbands. There were her dolls too, porcelain ones from Paris, a wooden Russian one with secrets inside and the rag one left caught up in the tangle of blankets. Who would play with them now? Then she saw herself dressed in the blue cotton trousers with matching tunic, moving from room to room, sitting for a moment with her grandmother before going into the larger room where the family gathered for their meals. She willed herself to walk around that room. She stopped before the cabinet with the silver pieces that had been in the family for generations. When she was very small her grandmother had taken the key and unlocked the glass door and lifted out the pieces. One by one she had handed them to Mahtab, letting her run her fingers over the intricate patterns

33

on the bowls and the carafes, telling her the story of how each came to be part of the family. For some time now the top shelf had been empty. Why hadn't she noticed that before? She turned to the bookshelf with its heavy, leather-bound volumes of Persian poetry, some belonging to her father, more to her grandfather from their student days. Would Uncle Wahid read them to his sons the way her father had read them to her? And finally to the wall with the photographs: Uncles Rahim and Karim who had gone to Paris, her great-grandparents, all of them now long dead. One grandfather and grandmother dead before the time of the Taliban and then her grandfather, gentle Grandpa, gone so cruelly, so recently. Mahtab could not bear to think of them. She wanted to take her mind on to the heavy wooden door and then out into the garden with the fruit trees, the wading pool, but instead it was all blank and again she wept.

Another time, she tried again. She would remember people. Ms Mahboubeh, her tutor, the young woman who had come to the house so bravely when schools and learning were closed to girls. Her brother had been taken to fight in the north with the army of the Taliban and she didn't know if he was alive or dead. Beneath her burqa she carried books but it was her face that Mahtab brought to mind: the huge dark eyes, filled with a determination to share what she knew with Mahtab and Leila, whatever the consequences. She had a mole on the side of her nose and a tiny scar on her cheek, got, she said, when she fell from an almond tree as a child. Mahtab could hear her voice, one minute reciting the poems, then gently correcting her pupils as they tried to imitate. How would she earn a living now?

~~~

One night as they travelled on in the darkness, there was a sudden lurching. The side of the truck seemed to fall away. There were shudders, the sound of gears dropping back and then they pulled off the track and stopped. Farhad and Soraya stayed sleeping as Mahtab and their mother joined their father and Jamal in the moonlight. He shrugged, shook his head and kicked the rear left tyre. It was shrivelled, sunken in the dust. 'We'll have to wait till morning. I'll change it then. We'll be all right here.' He climbed back into the cabin as the others pulled their blankets around their shoulders and huddled by the edge of the road.

After a few minutes, Mahtab's mother climbed back into the truck.

Mahtab stayed with her father. She looked up at the clear night sky. 'It's like the times when we used to go up on the roof at home,' she whispered. 'Remember? You used to let me sleep up there with

Leila and when I was really little you said the sky was a giant ceiling over us scattered with diamonds. And then you taught me that star was Castor and that one Pollux and the brightest group was the constellation the Great Bear. Will we be able to see them in Pakistan?'

Her father put his arm around her shoulders. 'Yes. The moon and the stars are constant. That's why we named you Mahtab: "moonlight".'

Mahtab wasn't sure what he meant but she nodded.

'Come on now, back in the truck. '

'Can't I stay a bit longer?' She leant against him. 'I'm warm here with you.'

'Just a few minutes then.' They sat together in silence.

'You know, Mahtab,' he said, after a while, 'it's a pity I didn't get you a diary. You're big enough to write down all the things that are happening, and then when you are as old as your grandmother you could tell your story to your grandchildren. They will want to know. Writing things down can be a help too, for you.'

Again Mahtab felt unsure of what he meant. Wouldn't writing about the bad things that might happen make the feeling worse? This time when he suggested she climb back into the truck, she stood up and whispered goodnight. At that moment, from somewhere high above them came a high, whining howl, then another.

Wolves.

'They are far away. They cannot hurt us here.'

But when Mahtab tried to sleep, she saw a confusion of whips, turbans and wild animals, their black hair streaked with grey, their jaws gaping, saliva dripping from their huge, jagged teeth.

~~~

In the morning, Mahtab's father and Jamal lifted the heaviest wardrobe from the truck and shifted other furniture forward. Then they pushed a huge jack under the frame of the tray and worked the lever up and down until the wheel was lifted free of the road. Farhad held the bolts while the wheel was pulled off and the spare one worked onto the hub in its place. The bolts were tightened, the truck lowered and air was pumped into the tyre.

All the while, Mahtab sat with her mother and Soraya in the shade of the truck, hidden from view of anyone on the hillside that ran down to a river valley. Flocks of sheep grazed the lower section of the mountain, splashes of white and grey set against the green. Mahtab saw the low black tents of the shepherds' families set out on the flat land, the valley floor. She glimpsed a child the size of Soraya, her clothing scarlet against the dull brown stones. As she leant forward, staring, trying to make out if there were other children, maybe her own age, her mother pulled her back. 'You must not be seen. Not even here.'

Mahtab's head dropped onto her knees. Her shoulders slumped. 'Are we ever going to get there?'

'We'll get there.' Her mother reached into the cotton bag on her lap. She took out a small spice jar and tipped from it the last grains of chilli.

'What are you doing?' Mahtab watched as her mother cleaned the chilli dust from the jar and then pressed the tiny container into the dirt beside the road. She lifted it, filled with grey and brown grains flecked with shiny sparkles of quartz.

'We'll get there,' said her mother again. 'And we will remember.'

~~~~

Two days later when they stopped for a break, Mahtab looked out over a wide valley. They were still up high and the road ahead of them hugged the mountains as far as the eye could see.

'Jamal tells me Pakistan is beyond that,' said her father, waving his hand at the rocky peaks ahead. 'We will be there tomorrow.'

'Good,' said her mother, 'we only have food for today.'

They made tea and dipped the stale bread in it and ate in silence. Just ahead of them, pushed off to the side of the road, was the remains of a tank, one side sunk in the dirt. The barrel of the gun was torn off and lying against a rock, and the hatch cover was gone. The gap left was burnt, black.

'Can I go and look?' Farhad finished eating, stood up and started to head towards it.

'Come back. Stay here,' his father said.

'But what is it? Why is it here?'

'It's a Russian one. Defeated in the end,' said Dad. 'Many people try to take over our country, but they never stay. Eventually they go, we beat them or they grow weary and return to where they belong.'

Will we return to where we belong? Where do we belong, now? Mahtab stared at the tiny ants crawling on the stalks of dead yellow grass at her feet. 'You are here for ever,' she whispered, 'but I am leaving.'

'We'll cross the border at around dawn,' said her father. 'Jamal has contacts who'll meet us there, so we should be all right. You'll have to stay quiet. You'll probably all be asleep.'

~~~

But Mahtab was awake when the truck drew up at the small concrete building. Through the narrow gap in the side of the truck she could see groups of people, men, women and children, bags and suitcases beside them, sitting on the side of the road. For maybe half an hour she was still and silent. Farhad and Soraya slept.

Then the truck inched forward. Stopped. A man's voice. He was so close, she felt she could reach from her hiding place and touch him. She concentrated, willing herself to hear what was said.

The language was strange. The man was talking, then Jamal. They moved away.

Was this truly the last time someone, anyone, could stop them, haul them from their hiding place, send them back to what lay behind them? Was the cage door about to open and she, the frightened bird inside, about to be set free? She clamped her hands over her mouth and drew her knees up to her chest. *Ninety-nine, ninety-eight, ninety-seven. Please, please, please let us through.* Her mother's lips were moving in prayer. *Ninety-six, ninety-five…* The truck door opened. Boots walked away. *Ninety-four, ninety-three, ninety-two…*

What lay ahead? What sort of life was there beyond this point? Pakistan? Australia? *Don't think about that. Just get through this.* More muffled voices. Long pause. Her mother's hand in hers. Squeezing. More waiting. Counting. Finally, footsteps returning, doors slamming, engine starting, wheels turning, truck moving.

We're through. We're through. Mum's hand squeezing harder. Crying. Crying. *Happiness and joy. Happiness and joy.*

Chapter Four

THEY RODE TOWARDS Quetta through fields of golden haystacks. Jamal had peeled back the tarpaulin and shifted the cabinets. Now Mahtab stood in the sunlight, the cool air on her face, her veil streaming behind her. The wind was cold but not the icy blasts of the mountains. This cold refreshed, and she felt a rosy glow to her cheeks. Two weeks of huddling, bent almost double and fearful, fell from her as dead leaves fall in winter. She was tall and strong and ready.

Her mother stood with her, smiling, her burqa thrown back to cover only her hair. Her eyes shone and the chain of gold coins around her neck sparkled in the sun. Seeing it, Mahtab pushed back

41

the sleeve of her tunic and let the sun gleam on her grandmother's bracelet.

They drew up, still some distance from the city. There was a farmhouse, enclosed by a high wall, and Jamal got out and banged loudly on the heavy wooden door. It opened and a man appeared and after a brief conversation came to the truck. Mahtab's father climbed onto the back. Jamal and the other man got into the cabin and the journey to the city started again.

'Who is he, Dad?' Farhad tugged at his father's shirt.

'A friend. He has arranged a house where we can stay. He has to guide us. Everything is all right.'

'Will there be a garden and a swing, like at home?'

'Possibly.'

'And will there be some boys to play with?'

'I don't know.'

'And something to eat? I'm hungry.'

'Me too,' said Soraya.

'And me,' said Mahtab. She was thinking of a bath, carpets and a bed; a soft, clean mattress, no dust, no dirt, no hard wooden planks to lie on, no bumping, grinding, bouncing over rough, half-made roads. Just a soft down mattress and she would lie on it and bury her face in it and sleep forever.

~~~

They stopped on a narrow street. Again Jamal beat on a heavy wooden door and this time he called the family to climb down and to bring all their belongings. They stood there in the dust until the door was opened by a huge, burly man with long hair and a thick beard who waved them in and then began a lengthy conversation with Mahtab's father.

There was no swing, no garden at all. Across the patch of bare dirt were two buildings, one a rambling collection of rooms, the other a shed. It was to this second building that the family was led.

Inside were two rooms. One contained a bed, the other a mattress and two cushions as well as a sink, kerosene stove and small cupboard. A narrow door led to a toilet outside. The floor was packed earth.

Jamal and the man they had picked up earlier shook hands with Mahtab's father and wished the family well.

The bearded man left too but he promised to return with food. The door closed.

Soraya began to cry.

'Stop it,' said her father. 'We have escaped. We are still alive. It is not like home but what does a little discomfort matter?'

'I'm going to call that man "Hairy Man,"' whispered Farhad.

Mahtab's mother filled the sink with water

and they took turns to wash their face and hands. The water, clean before Mahtab plunged her hands into it, turned almost to mud. Time and again the filthy water was drained away.

'I don't recognise you.' Dad cuffed Farhad behind the ear. 'This is a new face. A clean face. I don't know it at all.'

'And you're a stranger to me. Ah, Mum, there's a strange man here, protect me,' Farhad giggled.

Hairy Man returned with bread and yoghurt and fruit. He ate with them and spoke at length about the forward journey to Malaysia, Indonesia and Australia and of how in that country they would be free of the dangers they had known before. 'It is not a Muslim country,' he said, 'but there are many like us who have made it their home.'

'I know,' said Mahtab's father. 'I have heard and read about it.'

Mahtab knew he was thinking of the young man he had met so many years ago. That young man had told of the rich farmland he had lived on, fields of wheat like those they had just travelled through. The city where he had studied was new, newer than anything Mahtab could imagine, and it was built beside the sea. Where was he now?

'But you must go first,' the man said to Mahtab's father. 'It is better that way.'

Mahtab trembled. No. They had come so far together, because they *were* together.

'We will talk in the morning. My family is exhausted.' He poured more tea for them all. 'We are very grateful, but now we must pray and we must sleep.'

~~~

Sleep didn't come. Mahtab lay on the mattress and stared at Soraya and Farhad, curled up like puppies on the cushions. He must not leave them. What would happen to him? If they all stayed together, he was safe. She could hear her mother and father talking softly in the next room. If he went now, alone, journeying through strange countries, anything might... anyone might seize him again. The wind rattled the sheet of iron above her head. She heard strange insect sounds. And what would happen to them? How would Mum manage with no man to protect her? This was an unknown city. They had no friends, no family here. Mum had never been alone. Would Hairy Man look after them? Did he have a wife and children? Would he take all their money? Their gold jewellery? She ran her fingers over her bracelet, feeling the shallow indentations on the flat surfaces of the coins. Grandma had said the writing on them was in a language from India that she could not read or understand. All she knew was that it had been in the family, passed down for many, many years. What else had she said? *So you will always remember*.

Sleep must have come eventually because she woke to the sound of cups being put out and the smell of tea being poured. They sat on the floor and handed around the bread and talked of their plans.

'When we get to the place where we're going to live, Dad,' said Soraya, 'can I have a paddling pool like the one at home?'

'You can have everything you want, everything I can get for you.' Her father pulled her onto his lap. 'I'll talk to the men who arrange things this morning and we will set out as soon as we can.'

'In a truck?'

'No, little one. There will be all kinds of other ways to travel – a plane and a boat ... I'll find out what we have to do to get away as quickly as possible. This is not a good place to stay, even though it is safe and it's more comfortable than the truck. I want us all to leave together.'

He kept saying this for three days while the owner of the house and the many men who visited said otherwise. Mahtab sat on the mattress inside as they squatted in the yard and went over and over the route to be taken, the money that was needed, the

46

time and the dangers. Finally, her mother urged him to go ahead.

'Maybe they are right. Maybe it is more expensive than we ever imagined. Go quickly. Discover the way and then, when you are there and are able to send more money, we will come too. We are safe here. The man will bring food and I will keep the children here, with me. I will not let them go out into the streets or put themselves in harm's way. When you are safely there, you can send us word and tell us what we have to do.'

He was persuaded. Plans were made. Money changed hands. As the time drew closer, the family grew silent. Mahtab watched her father's every move. Her eyes followed him as he crossed the yard to meet with the strangers who came to instruct him. She noticed the way he tugged at his beard as he tried to make up his mind, the way he sucked his bottom lip in as he concentrated, the way he tossed his head back and laughed, showing the gaps where three teeth were gone on the left-hand side. She stared at the curly dark hair on the backs of his fingers as he lifted his tea to drink, and at his back, laced with the purple, bulging scars, as he stood half dressed.

Farhad and Soraya clung to him. They rode on his back or walked with their arms wound tightly around his waist. When he sat they lay on the floor, their heads resting on his legs.

On the last night they all spooned meatballs and rich spinach sauce onto the flat rounds of bread.

'I will not eat this well again until you are with me in Australia.' Their father wiped the spilt sauce from his beard and put his arm across his wife's shoulders. 'It will not be long.'

~~~

Later that night, when Farhad and Soraya slept, he knelt on the floor beside Mahtab's mattress.

'I pray that we will be all together again soon but you know that many things can happen and the journey is long. You are the eldest and you understand that the next few months will be very difficult for your mother. She will need your help. The others are too young to understand when they are in danger. They will get very bored here. There is nowhere to play as there was at home. There are no toys, no books, no friends. It will be up to you to help Mum as much as you can.' He put his arms around Mahtab and hugged her, tightly. 'Play games with them. Tell them stories. Talk to them of the things I have told you about Australia. Try to keep them as calm as you can.' He stroked her hair and kissed her forehead. 'We will be together again. We will be free, free from the fear and all that we have seen and we have suffered. I promise you that.'

How could she say to him what she was thinking? Without her watching over him, with him in strange lands, with strange men, so far away...Mahtab pushed these thoughts from her mind, wrapped her arms around him and pressed her face to his chest.

In the morning he was gone.

~~~~~

At first their days remained the same. They got up and washed and then Mahtab and her mother knelt in the second room to pray. They ate their morning meal and took turns imagining where their father might be and what he might be doing.

'He is sailing on the sea like Sinbad,' said Farhad. 'He can see lots of fish and there are giant whales as big as islands.'

'He is in the new country already,' said Soraya, 'and he has got us a house and there is a special room for each of us and an orange tree like the one we had before and the paddling pool for me is the biggest one in the whole world and soon he will tell us to come.'

Mahtab would tell them some of the things her father had told her that he had learnt from the young man from Australia. 'Everyone can have a television and you don't have to hide it away in a cupboard so that no one can find it.' And 'Everyone must go to school, even the girls, until they are fifteen and you cannot get married until you are eighteen,' and 'You can travel anywhere in the country, girls too, and there is not war and you are not scared that someone will take your money or your life.' To herself she said, *and I can study at the university like Grandma's sister and be a doctor.*

~~~

Weeks passed. The days grew longer and longer and they heard nothing of him. Everyone slept later. The hot sun was high above them as they drank the first tea of the morning. Then they pushed the mattress and the cushions back and that empty space became their world for the day. They talked less of him and more of their life before. They dredged up from their minds the memories of their home and their family, talking of Grandma, aunts and uncles and cousins until the pain of remembering became too great and they begged each other to stop. They cooked, taking time to mix flour and water and occasionally milk to prepare the dough for bread. Sometimes when Hairy Man delivered their food for the week there was meat, and then Mum would take her time and mix with it the spices she had carried across the border, firming the mixture into tight balls for cooking with vegetables. Whenever there was spinach sauce they thought back to that night, the night before their father left, when they had all eaten his favourite meal.

~~~

Weeks became months. Sometimes when they sat in the doorway with only the sunshine for company Farhad asked, 'Where is our father now? Why haven't we heard?'

Mahtab wasn't sure how to answer. She knew that Malaysia and Indonesia were to the east of Pakistan. She knew too that at some stage of the journey there was a sea to be crossed, but she didn't know the order they came in or how long any part of the journey would take. So she always said, 'He is still travelling.'

At times Farhad stood silently in the doorway, listening to the sounds of boys playing beyond the wall: running feet, a ball kicked and thudding against the bricks, eager cries.

'Let me go,' he said to his mother one day. 'Let me play with them.'

She said no, and he grew angry and took a stick and gouged deep holes in the ground. He stomped on dried leaves, shattering them into hundreds of tiny pieces, grinding them into the dirt. When his mother called him to stop he shouted back, 'Where is my father? Why did he go? He doesn't want us.' He pressed his face against the wall and would not look at anyone.

~~~

One day Hairy Man delivered paper and pencils along with the lentils and the green vegetables.

'I asked him for these,' Mum said. She took one sheet and drew a large square and then divided it up into many smaller squares.

'What is it?' Farhad was impatient.

'You'll see.' She coloured in every second square along the row.

Mahtab knew. 'It's a chessboard,' she whispered.

Her mother nodded. 'We'll make the pieces from paper too.'

They drew each piece of a chess set on the remaining paper and gently tore around the shapes: kings and queens, bishops, knights and rooks, and finally a whole collection of pawns.

'But I don't know how to play,' said Farhad.

'I'll teach you.' Mahtab remembered the nights at home when she used to sit beside her father and he pointed out to her the folly in a move she was about to make. He instructed her in the need to plan ahead, to think what move her opponent might be going to make and to find ways to escape that move. 'It's a game of the mind,' he said. 'A game of the mind.' That set, left behind in Herat, was made of marble. She tried to remember the cool feel of the rounded shapes in her hand and she wondered if anyone played with them now.

Every day after breakfast they lay on their bellies on the floor, pushing the tiny bits of paper from square to square, claiming their victories as each outmanoeuvred the other. It wasn't easy – a cough was enough to blow a piece from its place – but they persisted.

Gradually, Farhad's skill increased and even Soraya spotted moments when danger lurked for him. After an hour or so he would shrug his shoulders and announce that he had had enough. He stood at the open door and again begged their mother to let him go out, find some other boys to play with. Perhaps there would be a ball to kick around, a kite to fly.

She always said no.

Then it would be time for a story. Aladdin and His Lamp, Ali Baba, The Ebony Horse, Sinbad the Seaman. They knew them all, but they lay together across her bed and listened as the familiar words washed over them and took them out of the tiny room with its dark, bare walls and on to exotic lands.

~~~~

One day, Soraya and Farhad begged for a different story.

'You tell one,' Mum said to Mahtab. 'I want to lie down.'

'But I don't know any.'

'Yes you do.' Soraya climbed onto her sister's lap. 'There's nothing to do here.'

'Come on, Mahtab. You used to tell us good stories.'

'All right.' Mahtab thought for a moment. 'Once upon a time, there was a little girl called Soraya who had a brother called Farhad. They used to live in Herat but now they are bigger and they live under a different sky in a land called Australia. They have a wonderful house with a big garden with fruit trees that feed them, and they grow oranges so big and juicy that when they suck them the juice runs all over their chin. And there are delicious almonds and flowers too, bright, gorgeous flowers that delight them, and the sun is always shining and Farhad has a great big kite and he can fly it with the other children in the street.'

'What does Soraya have?' the little girl asked, nestling down, her head pressed against Mahtab's ribs so hard that they hurt. She placed her thumb in her mouth and sucked on it the way she had as a baby.

Mahtab remembered something her father had shown her in a book about Australia.

'She is very lucky. For her birthday her father has been to the market and he doesn't buy her a caged bird as he would in her old land. He buys her a kangaroo.'

'A kangar – what? What's that?'

'A kangaroo. It is one of the most amazing of all the creatures on Earth. It has a small face and a big body and a strong tail so it can stand up on its tail and its back feet. And it doesn't walk, it can't walk like a donkey or a camel. Its front paws are too little. It jumps. Everywhere. That's how it gets around. And the most special thing about it is that it has a pouch, here at the front.' Mahtab patted her stomach. 'And in that pouch it can put its babies and carry them around when it's looking for food.'

'A pocket?' Soraya giggled. She picked up her small rag doll and tucked it into the top of her trousers and danced across the floor. 'I'm a kang-ar-oo. I'm a kang-ar-oo.' She was laughing. Farhad too. He picked up a sandal and tucked it into his pants. He jumped from the mattress across to the door and back and suddenly they were all laughing and rolling on the floor as if they were happy again in their own house, in their own land.

~~~

Later, their giggling done, Farhad said, 'If they have such funny animals there, maybe the people are funny too and they have three legs.'

'Or two heads,' said Soraya.

'Or their eyes are at the back of their head.'

'Their two heads.'

Their giggling started again. Mahtab didn't join

them. She knew there would be things that were different, Dad had told her. But what would it really feel like, to go to school, to study, to try to find a friend?

That night when the younger children were asleep, Mahtab lay on the bed with her mother. 'Do you think he is still travelling?'

'I don't know,' her mother said. 'I lie here at night trying to picture where he is. But I know nothing of the world. I have never been anywhere but Herat. I don't know what those places he talked of look like. I don't know how far away they are or how wide the ocean is that he has to cross. He told me much of the way he would go but I can't remember it all.'

'How long is it since he left?'

'Five months. He must be there by now.'

'So why doesn't he call us? He said that he'd phone.'

'I don't know. I just don't know.'

After that, Mahtab didn't ask again. She sat all day on the floor or on the mattress, sometimes occupying her thoughts with memories of the past or imaginings of the future. More often, her mind was blank. When she got up to go into the other room, she moved slowly, her limbs heavy. She saw her mother was the same. They grew pale and quiet. It felt as if only Farhad and Soraya had any life in them. They still giggled as they played the kangaroo game, seeing which one could jump higher and further, which one could stuff the most sandals and shoes into their pouch. Once when Hairy Man came to deliver their weekly food, they demanded he watch and judge which of them made the better creature. He shook his head and hastened away even more quickly than usual.

Chapter Five

ONE WEEK INTO their eighth month without their father, Hairy Man knocked on the door and called their mother out to talk with him. He spoke curtly to Mahtab, insisting that she stay inside.

When their mother returned, she brushed Soraya away and went straight into the other room, drawing the curtain across the doorway.

After a few moments, Mahtab followed her.

'What is it? Has something happened to our father? Is everything all right?'

'No. Nothing has happened to your father and no, everything is not all right.' She was frowning, her hands in her lap, twisting her rings till they pressed hard into the skin of her fingers.

'What are you talking about?'

'Sit down.' She patted the space beside her on the bed. 'You're a big girl now, Mahtab. I need you to understand exactly what is going on and what we will have to go through. The man has just told me of something very worrying. There are others – people fleeing Afghanistan who are in safe houses and in refugee camps in this district. Lots are like us – the husband and father has gone first and the mother and the children are waiting for money to begin their next stage of travelling. Now there is a gang that has decided the men who are in Australia already must have money, so they are kidnapping the women and children and holding them hostage. They take them off into the tribal lands and no one knows exactly where they are. The police don't care. The government doesn't care. They just want money – the money which was for travel is paid to these brigands to buy the family's freedom.'

Brigands. The robbers of Ali Baba, the cut-throat thieves and murderers of every story she had ever heard. She felt the heavy ice stone sink into her stomach again. 'What can we do? Will they come for us?'

'I don't know.'

'What did Hairy Man think?'

'He says we should stay out of sight. He doesn't think anyone knows we are here.'

'Do you trust him?'

'I have to.'

'I wish Dad would write or phone.'

'So do I. For now it's even more important that we stay inside, away from any visitor who comes.'

~~~

For days, their mother insisted the children stay as quiet as possible. She refused to explain when challenged by Farhad and Soraya, saying only that she did as she did for good reason. Mahtab jumped at any noise from the yard outside. The slamming of a door, the barking of a dog, the call of a strange voice sent her to retreat to the second room, curtain drawn. She drew her brother and sister to her and whispered to them anything she could remember about Australia.

'In Australia we will not have to stay inside all the time. You, Farhad, will play football whenever you want to and girls too can play. No one will tell us that we must be quiet all the time. We will all go to school and play games, new games too that we don't even know of yet. And many of our teachers will be women like Ms Mahboubeh but they will not be sad and their brothers will not have disappeared.

Our father told me that we will be as surprised as he is at all the things we can do. You can fly kites every day, in the garden or in the public park like Dad did when he was young, and no one will try to stop you.'

'Does anything bad happen in Australia?' asked Soraya.

'I don't think so.' Mahtab paused. 'Dad said that sometimes there are robbers and maybe even a murderer but then the government doesn't hang them or shoot them, they put them in jail for ever and ever.'

'What a strange place,' Farhad said.

A strange place. Mahtab rolled the words around in her mind. Strangers in a strange land. Their father had said so much more than she had told the others. Weird things like young girls in public with their hair and shoulders uncovered and young people out without their parents to guide them. When she asked if she would have to do these things, he had laughed and said of course not. She would still be her parents' daughter and she would do as they wished.

'Do you wish me to study hard?' she had asked.

He had nodded. 'That I do, but it will not be easy. First, you will have to learn English.'

'Will that be difficult?'

'I believe so. I cannot be sure. I have heard it but I do not speak it myself.'

~~~

61

On the third night after the conversation with her mother, Mahtab couldn't sleep. She waited until Farhad and Soraya's breathing grew deeper and then she knelt beside the bed and whispered urgently, 'Mum, can I talk to you about something?'

'Of course.'

'We may be in danger from those that you told me of, right?'

'Yes. I believe so.'

'And we have not heard from my father.'

'No.'

'Well, why don't we follow him? Hairy Man can tell us what we have to do. He can organise things the way he did for Dad. I don't want to stay here.'

'We have to stay here. I don't like it any more than you do, but your father said that when he was settled he would contact us and then we could follow.'

'But what if...'

'No *what if*s. We will hear from him in time. There is nothing we can do. Now go to sleep.'

Mahtab crept back to her mattress but sleep did not come. What if Dad was not settled? What if he was never settled? What if something had happened to him when he was in one of the countries he had to cross? He could be like Sinbad, wrecked by whales or giant waves. She squeezed her eyes shut, trying to picture his face in those days before he left, the smile as he had held her tightly on that last evening. *We will be together again, I promise you that.* Could he keep that promise?

The next morning Mahtab played with her breakfast. She tore the dried bread into strips and rolled one into a ball before finally putting it into her mouth. She threaded another through her fingers and nibbled at the edges that hung over her palm. She let her tea go cold.

'Come on, eat up.' Her mother frowned.

'Why? Are we going somewhere?' She had never spoken to her mother in that voice before.

~~~

Later Mahtab spread her possessions on the mattress: two sets of underclothes, a nightdress, thin now and reaching only just below her knees, two shirts, two pairs of socks, a second pair of trousers, a second veil, a hairbrush and a small hand towel. She packed them back into her small bag, leaving out the photo of Leila.

'What's this?' Farhad grabbed it and held it up to the light.

'Give it back.' She snatched the photo from him and ducked behind the curtain, into the darkened room of her mother.

'What is it now?'

'Look. He took my photo of Leila. He's torn the corner of it. I hate him. He should leave my things alone.'

'He's just bored, Mahtab. It's hard for everyone.'

'That's why we should go. We'll go mad shut up in this place.'

'Don't talk like that.'

'But it's true.'

'We are not going and I don't want to hear you speak of it again.'

~~~

And then Farhad was gone. Mahtab and her mother came out of the inner room and saw Soraya drawing with three pencils in one hand.

'Look what I can draw.'

'Where is Farhad?'

'Outside.'

But when they peered through the doorway they saw only the empty yard.

'Did you see him?' Their mother seized Soraya's shoulders.

The little girl shook her head.

'Did you see anyone come into the yard?'

'No.'

'Did you hear anyone? Anything?'

Mahtab watched her mother pacing the tiny room. She could feel that tightening again, fear squeezing her stomach, closing her throat. 'I could look outside,' she said, 'outside the wall.'

'No, not you.' Her mother grabbed her cloak. 'I'll go.'

Mahtab and Soraya waited.

'Have the black-turban men got Farhad?' said Soraya.

'Don't be silly, they aren't here.'

'Where is he then?'

Mahtab didn't answer.

For hours they waited. One minute Mahtab paced up and down the length of the two rooms, the next she flopped on the bed and buried her face in her hands. What if Mum couldn't find him? What if he never came back? What if she was lost too? If she never returned? Could she, Mahtab, go on? Could she find her father? Soraya climbed up on the bed beside her. She put her arms around Mahtab's neck and the two of them lay silent for a long, long time.

~~~~

And then they were there, Farhad crying, pushed into the yard by his mother. She gripped his arm, yelling, 'How dare you disobey me. You don't know who those boys are. I have told you that there is danger to you, to all of us, if some people know we are here. Do you want us dead? Go into the inner room and stay there.'

~~~~

Mahtab sat under the sink, her back pressed hard against the wall. She stared at the photo of Leila. Was she safe now, in Iran? Was she with her mother and her father and her older sister? Was she going to school? Was she taller too, like Mahtab, her wrists poking out of the folded cuffs of her tunic? Would they ever see each other again?

Soraya came and sat opposite her. 'What are you doing?'

'Nothing.'

'Come and play a game with me?'

'No.'

'Why not?'

'I don't want to.'

'Don't you like me?'

'Not today.'

Soraya's bottom lip curled and tears welled in her eyes.

'Don't cry. Mum'll get angry.'

'Play with me then.'

Mahtab crawled out from under the sink and pushed the photo back into her bag. 'What do you want to play?'

'Drawing. It's not really a game. We just have to draw.' She pointed to sheets of paper in the corner and produced two pencils from her pocket. 'I'm drawing Mumma and my paddling pool and the orange tree.'

'I'll draw our old house,' said Mahtab as she took a sheet of paper. She drew quickly – the long outside brick wall broken by the heavy double doors. Above them the inner building, a single storey with sections jutting into the garden, the fruit trees, the trailing creepers that spread under the windows. She drew the detail, the fine narrow leaves, the bursting flowers. She glanced at her little sister. Soraya had stopped drawing and was staring at her.

'What's the matter?'

'When did Daddy die?'

'What?'

'When did Daddy die?'

'He didn't. He's not dead.'

'He must be. Where is he?'

Mahtab rocked forward and back. She turned the pencil slowly in her hand. Farhad was still in the other room with her mother. She took a long, deep breath. 'Hasn't Mum told you? He got in touch with Hairy Man. He has arrived safely and he's sending money and we are leaving soon to go and be with him. There was danger, but he is safe. You mustn't tell Mum that I told you. She hasn't told Farhad either. She is very happy but she gets all upset when she talks about it. She wants it to be a secret till we are ready to go.'

'Can I tell Farhad?'

Mahtab nodded. 'But he can't say anything to Mum. Promise?'

'I promise.' She grinned. 'Now I'm going to draw Dadda and a big whale.'

Mahtab watched her. How easily she believed. If only it were true.

That night, Mahtab again crawled into her mother's room and knelt beside her. 'Mum?'

'Mmmm.'

'Mum, I have to talk to you. Soraya thinks that Dad is dead. She asked me today when he died.'

'What? What did you say?'

'I told her it wasn't true but she doesn't believe me. We cannot stay here. We have to follow him. We have to.'

Her mother sat up. Her dark hair, streaked with grey at the temples, hung almost to her waist. She drew her cloak around her shoulders and clasped her hands together, fingers interlaced, and placed them in her lap, saying nothing.

'Well?' said Mahtab. She thought of telling her mother what else she had said to Soraya, but she pushed that from her mind.

Still her mother said nothing.

'Do you think he's dead?'

Her mother shook her head.

'We have to go, Mum. What if the bandits get us

or if something has happened to Dad and he cannot send us the money? We cannot stay here like this. We cannot.'

'Go to bed, Mahtab. I have to think about this. We'll talk in the morning.'

~~~

Mahtab woke to the sound of Farhad and Soraya giggling and sipping tea. They were sitting in the sunshine that filled the doorway. Their mother was gone.

'She's talking to Hairy Man,' said Farhad. 'She said we're going to follow Dad.' He stood up and ran around the room, arms outstretched. 'We're going on a big plane, brmm brmm.'

'I told him,' said Soraya. 'He said he won't tell Mum. He promised.'

They watched their mother come back across the dusty yard. She sat cross-legged on the mattress and they sat in front of her.

'He says we need papers: passports. That means photographs, so this morning we are going to the bazaar to have them taken. It's risky going out, but we can't travel without them. You are to wash and be ready in half an hour.'

~~~

In the van, Mahtab pressed her face to the window. She was outside the gate for the first time since they had arrived in Pakistan. She could see open fields, then clusters of farmhouses and beyond them, far in the distance, the mountains of her homeland, Afghanistan. Shivers ran through her body. What of those who had taken the women and children hostage? Could that happen, today? Today when they were finally making the plans to leave?

~~~~

'Stay very close,' Mum said as they climbed down from the van. 'Especially you, Farhad. Don't look anybody in the eye and don't stop to touch or to look at anything.' She held on tightly to Soraya's hand as they walked beneath the arched doorway.

They were in the meat market. Carcasses of cows, goats and sheep hung from hooks above them. Men stood behind broad benches, trimming cuts of meat, brushing aside the fat and wrapping the bloody chunks that a buyer had chosen. Chickens, live ones, squawked and flapped as their necks were wrung and they were thrust head-first into shopping bags. Live birds, not destined for the table, called and sang as Hairy Man led the family further into the maze of stalls.

~~~~

Mahtab kept her eyes on the worn flagstones as they passed brilliantly rich carpets, burnished copper utensils, huge buckets filled with objects of tin and plastic.

'Hey, girl. A dress for you? A scarf?'

She ignored the young man calling from his racks of brightly coloured cotton shirts, trousers and dresses. The smell of spices washed over her and from the corner of her eye she saw huge tubs of gleaming peppers, golden turmeric, cinnamon and cardamom and others that she didn't know. More voices called to them to buy, but they stayed close to Hairy Man and hurried on. At length he turned down a narrow alley, opened a door and then led them into a dark room.

~~~

They sat on a bench, waiting while a man and his three sons were photographed. Then one by one they went behind a curtain and climbed onto a high stool. Mahtab went first. She sat as still as she could, her hands in her lap, her face frozen, neither smiling, nor frowning. Her eyes were fixed on the camera. *We are coming, Dad. We are coming.*

They left quickly, retracing their steps, past the spices, the clothing, the carpets, and then the birds and meat. Only when they had reached the van did they stop. They fell into their seats.

'Why don't we stay?' said Soraya. 'I'm hungry. I want something to eat.'

'No. We have to go.' Mahtab glanced around. Men lounged in shop doorways or squatted on the footpath, watching as Hairy Man slammed the van door and started the engine.

'I'll pick up the papers in a few days,' he said to their mother. 'You won't need to go back in there.'

'And the plane tickets?'

'Those too. You could be out of here in a week. Off to Malaysia.' He grinned at Farhad. 'Off in an aeroplane, eh?'

Mahtab tried to imagine it. Trucks she knew, and now vans. But an aeroplane. What would it be like to fly higher than a kite or a bird and further than any creature, ever? As they bounced over the rough surface of the road, she tried to see herself looking down on the world, from the window of her plane. What would mountains and deserts, villages and towns be like from up there? Would people seem as small as the ant she could squash beneath her sandal?

~~~~~

At home, when the others were asleep, Mahtab lay on the mattress next to her mother.

'I'm glad we're leaving here. Where exactly are we flying to?'

'Malaysia first. Then we have to take a second plane to Indonesia. The man says that we must fly over the sea. You will see the sea for the first time.'

'What's it like?' Mahtab snuggled in closer to her.

'I'm not sure. I haven't seen it either. Some say it is as blue as the sky on a clear summer day, some say green like the dense glass in a bottle.'

'And there will be fish?'

'And seagulls.'

'What are they?'

'Special sea birds that follow the fish as they move around and dive down and eat them.'

'And when we get there, I wonder if Dad will be there?'

'Not in Indonesia. We'll take a boat then and cross more sea, and finally, finally, we'll get to Australia. That's where your father has gone.'

Mahtab rolled over then and hugged her mother. For the first time she saw that the necklace of gold coins was gone.

~~~~

Four nights later, they left for Malaysia. They set out for the airport just as the last rays of sun caught the tops of the mountains. They left nothing behind. Mahtab folded the paper chessboard and slipped it and the fragile pieces into the pocket on the inside of her bag. The few clothes they had brought were thinner and more faded than she had realised. Hairy Man's wife, Neeman, pressed a parcel of dried fruit into their mother's hand.

'For the trip,' she whispered and waved them

goodbye from her doorway as the van moved through the gate.

They drove in silence for about half an hour. The road took them past farms and along a flat area beside the river. As they turned from it and headed towards a cluster of buildings, a rumbling, roaring sound tore through the air. Above them, seemingly so low that they could reach up and touch it, was an aeroplane, lights winking, coming in lower, closer. Soraya grabbed Mahtab's hand and held it tightly, saying nothing.

~~~

At the airport, there were as many people as in a crowded marketplace. Children sat on battered suitcases or bags tied together with thin strands of rope. They waited while parents queued at ticket counters. Tired old men and women dozed on the floor. Mahtab heard voices, some raised in anger in languages she didn't understand. Men waved pieces of paper and shook their fists in the direction of officials behind the counters.

'I'll go there,' said her mother. 'You watch your brother and sister.'

Farhad and Soraya dragged Mahtab to the window to peer out at planes lined up in front of the wall like bulls at a feeding trough.

'Which one's ours?' Soraya pointed. 'That one?'

74

'That's a helicopter, stupid.' Farhad waved towards the sleeker commercial planes. 'One of them, probably, and we'll go right up, just like a bird.' He let go of his sister and pressed his nose against the glass. Then he turned back. 'No. We'll be like a kite, like the one we buried that day. Remember?'

Mahtab nodded. She saw again the beautiful red-and-blue fabric as the clods of brown earth rained over the boys' most precious things. And Leila. Was she safe? Did she remember? Uncle Wahid's screaming echoed in her head. 'We will all be killed. You are never to play like this again. Never. Never. Never.'

Soraya tugged her arm. 'Are all these people coming with us?'

Mahtab shrugged. 'I don't know. Maybe some of them.' She looked across the room. How many were from her country? How many had come as she had done, hidden, frightened, hoping? And what would come next?

Their mother found them and led them along a narrow passageway. They stood in line, waiting at the door of the plane.

'Can it really fit all these people?' whispered Soraya.

Mahtab nodded. 'I suppose so.'

They moved forward then, into the narrow tube

of the plane. A smiling woman guided them down the aisle and waved them to their seats: two on one side and two on the other. Mahtab found herself next to a window, glancing out at the lights of the terminal. The plane filled.

Farhad was strangely quiet. They all were. Their eyes never strayed from the person who first of all showed them how to click the belts that went across their laps. She pulled a yellow jacket over her head and said something as she tightened it and touched strange objects that hung from it. Mahtab couldn't quite understand the words she was saying but the meaning was clear. The woman took the jacket off and then sat down and tightened her own seatbelt. Calm words came over the loudspeakers.

The plane moved slowly back from the building and Mahtab looked out boldly, but when the engines roared like an angry lion and the plane lurched down the long road, they all seized each others' hands and Mahtab heard her mother praying. She closed her eyes and began the slow count backwards again.

Chapter Six

MAHTAB WOKE as a voice came over the loudspeakers. The sky outside was streaked with a pale golden light.

'Are we there yet?' whispered Soraya.

'I don't know.'

The plane shuddered. They heard screaming engine sounds, then a thud and groaning beneath them. Mahtab saw mountains and then huge city buildings, their glass throwing sunlight back into her eyes.

They bounced and slowed along the ground and she looked out at the rich green of the trees and shrubs beyond the fence of the airport.

Inside the terminal, they stayed close to each other, drawn along like flowing liquid. Signs were in writing Mahtab couldn't read. A small, smiling woman in a uniform as sharp as glass glanced at their tickets and barred their way from the main hall. She waved them through an opening into a room where there were already others sitting around with tired, waiting faces. There were no seats left, so they sat on the floor, in the corner by a window. Farhad and Soraya looked out at the planes but Mahtab pushed close to her mother. 'Where are our bags? What's happening now?'

'Someone told me the bags will be there when we arrive. For now, we wait.'

'For what?'

'For a plane to Indonesia.' Her mother closed her eyes.

~~~~

They sat that way for hours. The dried fruits were long gone and Mahtab became more and more hungry. Soraya and Farhad crawled on their mother's legs, one minute asking for food, the next demanding to know when they would be getting onto the next plane. Mahtab studied the rest of the group. They were mainly women with children, none her age. The chair opposite her was filled by a young woman with a boy the same size as Farhad. He had been sleeping, his cheek red from where it had rested on her round, pregnant belly. She saw Mahtab looking at her and she smiled in a tired, sad way.

The doors opened and another woman in the same severe uniform waved the group along a narrow corridor that stretched the length of the building. They walked slowly, Mahtab carrying Soraya as her mother spoke with other travellers, trying to find out what exactly was happening next. No one knew. They came to a door and a man in a uniform waited in front of it, seated behind a small desk. Each person held their papers.

~~~

The line moved as slowly as a lazy tortoise. Mahtab felt the muscles in her throat tighten. Ice stone in the belly again. Trapdoor throat. She stared at the people around her. Were they each as scared as she was? Would the man let them through? What if he took their papers and would not give them back?

The man in the uniform took the papers from the woman in front of them. He held them up to the light as if checking for some detail that wasn't immediately visible. He leant forward and spoke to the woman. She shrugged and said nothing. Mahtab lowered Soraya to the floor. Were all those papers false too? Did they also say that the bearer was Turkish and travelling for a holiday? The man in the bazaar in

Pakistan had told Mahtab's mother that this was the best way. It was the way her father had done it. The line moved forward. Mahtab whispered to Farhad and Soraya, 'Don't say a word.'

They rolled their eyes.

The man took the papers Mum handed him. He flicked through them and said something to her in a low voice that Mahtab couldn't understand.

She replied and he turned back to the papers and went through them more slowly. One by one he held them up, turned them over and placed them back on the desk. Then he shook his head.

How could he? Mahtab whispered a prayer. If he said they couldn't go on this plane, where would they go? What would they do? They could not go back. They could not stay here. They knew no one. Ahead of them, people were disappearing through the door and down another long corridor. Mahtab wanted to push the barrier aside and run after them.

The man coughed and made a gesture with his hand. Mahtab's mother nodded and reached into the pocket of her coat.

Money. It was money he wanted. It was what they all wanted. He knew precisely where they were from.

One of his hands curled around the notes her mother placed on the table, the other brought the stamp down on the papers.

They gathered up their bags and followed the others into the long, dark corridor.

~~~

This aeroplane was smaller than the previous one. It was parked out on its own and Mahtab and the other passengers had to walk along a yellow line, past larger, sleeker planes decorated with pictures of purple and yellow flowers. One had red circles and another one had strange green and blue symbols that Mahtab couldn't understand. The wind swirled the women's long cloaks around their legs. A metal staircase led to the front door and it shuddered under the heavy tread of the man ahead of Mahtab as she pulled herself up. Inside, the men all had to duck their heads and even Mahtab could touch the roof when she stretched up her hand.

The roar of the take-off this time was not that of an angry lion but Mahtab still found herself clutching the armrest and beginning her counting. *Ninety-nine, ninety-eight, ninety-seven* . . . As the plane climbed higher and higher she slackened her grip and lost track of the numbers. Had her father flown on this same plane? Had he got this far? Had he gone further? What would he think if he knew that they were in the air, kites with no string? She closed her eyes and pictured his face. He said he might shave his beard off once he got to Australia. What would he look like? Would she know him?

The plane shuddered. It vibrated from side to side as if it really was a kite and the boy controlling it was running first one way and then another, tugging and releasing it into the air, then calling it back. As if a giant cat was swiping at them like a ball of wool. Then the plane dropped. Mahtab's stomach leapt to her throat. Farhad grabbed her hand. Soraya cried out. From all over the plane came the sound of children crying and adults praying.

'Allah o Akbar. God is great.'

Up and down, side to side, the plane lurched its way in the darkness. Mahtab clutched at the armrest, digging her fingernails into the vinyl surface.

Dad. Dad. Why did you leave us? Why did I persuade Mum to leave Pakistan? A luggage rack ahead of her burst open and bags of clothes tumbled forward. The attendant who had been walking up and down calming the passengers sat down on the floor.

'Are we going to crash?' whispered Farhad.

'I don't know.'

The voice of the captain came on then, calm and matter-of-fact, but he was speaking in a language that no one understood and so the crying and the wailing continued.

Every few minutes the tossing of the plane lessened, the sounds inside quietened and Mahtab felt the pressure of Farhad's fingers die away. Her stomach settled back into its normal position. Then it would begin again, the feeling that they were a tiny scrap of metal being blown around by a great wind or a creature taking pleasure in the game.

In front of Mahtab was the woman travelling with her young son. Mahtab heard the deep guttural sound of her being sick, the splashing of whatever had been in her stomach hitting the floor. Her own stomach was empty and for once she was relieved.

Finally the shuddering and bouncing stopped.

Mahtab realised that the plane was now continuously level. The captain's voice came on again and the attendant got up and began moving around, picking up the clothes and belongings and cleaning the floor.

'Look,' said Farhad, 'look.' He pointed through the window and Mahtab could see, far below in the moonlight, an expanse of water and on it the dark shapes of ships. 'That's where we'll be.'

~~~

Mahtab had never seen such dark green. She peered from the window of the plane as it slowed and edged across the runway. Green everywhere: trees beyond the fence, shrubs in huge pots along the front of the building and closely clipped grass along the edge of the tarmac.

A tall, bearded man in Arab dress met them. He

wore a gold watch at his wrist and gold rings on four of his fingers. He spoke only to the three men from Iraq who were with the group and they in turn spoke to their wives, who passed the messages along to the women who travelled without husbands.

'He's taking us to a hotel,' said Mum. 'We're all going on the boat in a few days and there will be more people too.'

'I'm starving,' said Farhad.

'Me too.' Soraya tugged at her mother's hand.

'We'll just have to wait. I'm sure there'll be food when we get there.' She turned to talk further with the other women.

'Let's play a game.' Mahtab crouched down beside her younger sister and brother. 'I must be the cook and I've told you that you can have whatever you want in the whole world and I'll cook it for you. Doesn't matter how much it costs or anything.'

'Kebab,' said Farhad. 'Juicy, dripping kebab with tomatoes and lettuce and bits of onion and lots of bread and some sauce.'

'Meatballs,' said Soraya. 'With yummy sauce that's got all Grandma's special things in it and there's lots of bread to soak up everything and there'll be rice too, yellow rice and yoghurt, we forgot yoghurt.'

'Yes, yoghurt,' said Farhad, 'and you can have some too, Mahtab.' He rubbed his stomach. 'And there'll be tea and maybe a big, big bit of watermelon at the end.'

'Apples,' Soraya stretched her hands wide, 'this many apples from the tree at home and we can chop them up with more yoghurt.' She dropped her hands and the smile left her face. 'But I'm hungry now, and you're just pretending.' She cried then and Mahtab put an arm around her. Soraya's head rested on her shoulder. Farhad stood silently watching.

~~~~

They were led out to a bus which drove along a road high above the surrounding land. Mahtab looked down on pools of water: water on open fields, water around houses, water flowing down gutters. Then they were off the high road and driving through streets choked with traffic: cars, trucks and motorbikes. Mahtab stared at women in tight trousers riding on the backs of the bikes, their bare arms clasped tightly around the waist of the man in front of them, their hair loose and flying behind them. How could they do that? Would it be like this in Australia? Bicycles weaving their way in and out of the traffic, huge buildings with their tops disappearing above the level of the window. They stopped then started. Stopped again. Horns blared. Only the bicycles and people moved. Farhad pressed his nose against the glass and pointed and laughed.

Then they were off again, pushing their way through this sea of people.

They turned off the road and drove along a gravel path and through a large gateway. Gardens, dense with scarlet and golden flowers big enough to shelter birds, lined the drive up to a stone building. It was surrounded by wide verandahs with striped coloured blinds that flapped in the spaces between the stone columns.

Farhad leapt up but Mahtab sat staring at the gardens, drinking in the colour as the group stood and began to take down luggage and file along the centre of the bus. She was the last to leave.

At the front office their mother was given a metal ring with a key and a wooden token with a number burnt into it. They walked down a cool, tiled hall and then onto one of the wide verandahs. In front of them was a small courtyard and to their right the room that was to be theirs. It was huge, larger than any room Mahtab had seen. They kicked off their sandals and dropped their bags on the floor. They stretched out on the beds beneath a fan that turned slowly, moving cool air over their sticky bodies.

'I'm going to lie here and never ever get up again,' said Mahtab.

'Not even for food?' Mum pushed herself up on her elbow. 'There is a meal waiting for us in half an hour.'

'Maybe for food.'

They washed and changed and then found their way back around the verandahs and through the halls to the dining area. Steaming rice and vegetables were served. They ate quickly, glancing around at those they'd travelled with and many strangers as well.

After the meal, Mahtab sat in the courtyard outside their room. She trailed her fingers in the small rock pool, letting her hand be carried by the water and brush against the dangling fern fronds. Tiny golden fish darted between the rocks. Ruby-red flowers lined a narrow path of stones that led to the other side of the space.

Had Dad stayed here? Had he sat like this, staring into the water, thinking of his children as she sat thinking of him? Where was he now? Why hadn't he called? What had happened to him?

Chapter Seven

AFTER BREAKFAST, Mahtab's mother stayed with the other adults in the dining room to speak to the man who had met them at the airport. Mahtab took Soraya and Farhad and went towards the door.

'Can Ahmad come too?' Farhad waved to the boy who stood holding onto his mother's leg. She was the pregnant woman who had been ill on the plane.

Mahtab nodded and Farhad called the boy, who could have been his twin: the same straight hair that fell into his eyes, arms burnt brown from the sun, a grin that showed a tiny chip on one of his front teeth.

The boys lay, heads together on the tiles beside the rock pool.

'We're going on a big boat soon,' said Ahmad.

'We are too,' Farhad was quick to reply.

'And we're going to meet my dad.'

'So are we.'

'Maybe our dads know each other and they'll come and meet us.'

'Maybe we'll live in the same street. And we'll go to school together and we can get kites and play with them.'

'My kite will cut yours.'

'No. Mine will win. Your kite will fly away as high as our plane.'

The two boys rolled onto their backs in the warm sun and followed the clicking movements of geckos that crawled along the rafter above them.

After about an hour, their mother joined them.

'The agent has gone to organise the boat,' she said. 'He is from Egypt and he says he does this all the time. He says we can go in a week.'

'What do we do for the next week?' said Farhad.

'You boys can play – run around, burn off your energy,' said their mother. 'I'm going to get clean and rest. Ahmad's mother has already gone to lie down. She needs to relax. Her baby will come in a month or so.'

~~~

That night, Mahtab woke to a frightened calling and banging on the door. Ahmad stood there in the darkness, cheeks tear-stained. 'Mumma, Mumma,' he cried.

'What is it?' Soraya sat up on her bed, rubbing her eyes, as their mother spoke to the boy in a low voice and dressed quickly. She left with him but was back in minutes.

'That baby isn't waiting for Australia. I'm going with her to the hospital. Look after the children, Mahtab.'

They waited all through the night. At first Mahtab tucked them in together in her mother's bed, but when they refused to sleep she hugged them tightly and told them a story.

'There is a little baby,' she said, 'born in Australia and its mumma is very tired because she has so many other babies to look after so the dadda in the family decides that he will buy a kangaroo and it will be the one to carry the baby in its pocket. So, every morning, the mumma feeds the baby and she wraps that baby up and she puts him in the kangaroo's pocket and the kangaroo stays out in the sunshine and the little baby is as warm as if it was a loaf of bread just out of the oven. When he's hungry the kangaroo knows and brings the baby to the chair where that mumma is resting and she feeds him again and then just pops him back in.'

'Is that kangaroo gentle?' asked Soraya, sleepily.

'It's the gentlest nursemaid in the world.'

'My dadda will do just that,' said Ahmad.

~~~~

The children slept then. Mahtab watched over them, her head filled with the strange animal she had spoken of. Where did these crazy stories come from? Were there really creatures like that out there? Was there really the place her father had told her of? Was it the stuff only of story?

~~~~

In the morning their mothers had still not returned. No one spoke to them at breakfast. No one asked where their mothers were. When they had finished, they wandered along the corridors, not going directly to their own rooms but trying to take in the whole building. Mahtab said the numbers of the rooms in her head as she walked. They were working backwards from number one hundred and eighty and into her mind flashed the lurching of the truck, the slamming of doors, the crunching of gravel, the cold, cold feeling of her stomach tightening and the muscles in her throat closing over.

She started to run then, through the corridor out onto a verandah and around the edges of the building, past courtyards, past huge pots of purple creeper, past surprised old women sweeping the stones with their straw brooms. The others raced after her, calling her to stop, but she kept on running until she reached their own room, number sixty-one, and she dropped onto the warm sunlit tiles.

She was still there, sticky in the heat, when her mother came back.

'The baby is fine and Hamida is too,' she said. 'It's been a long night.'

'Where's my mumma?' Ahmad's face was all wrinkled as if he was about to cry.

'She's resting in the hospital.' Mahtab's mother pulled the boy onto her lap. 'And you have a baby sister, a beautiful little girl.'

'I wanted a brother.'

'You wait till you see her. She's so gorgeous. And your mum told me to give you a big hug and a kiss.' She pulled him closer and pressed her lips against his cheek.

Ahmad pushed himself away from her. 'Chase me. Come on,' he called to Farhad.

~~~

Mahtab made tea then and she and her mother sat on the woven matting, sipping from the glass cups.

'That new baby brings joy.' Mum put her glass down and fanned herself with the end of her scarf. 'All of that family are gone except Hamida and her husband, who is in Australia.'

'All dead?'

'All dead.' Her shoulders dropped and she let out a long sigh.

Mahtab knew that her mother was thinking of her family and of Grandpa. In her mind, she saw again the days and days of weeping and crying when that death came. She heard the anxious whispering and the conversations cut short whenever she entered the room and she knew the fear in her parents' faces as they talked of their long journey ahead. Most of all she remembered her silent father, the bruises on his face and chest, the raised welts on his back.

'Mum, where do you think Dad is?'

'I don't know.'

'Do you think something terrible has happened to him?'

'I don't want to think about that. Let's think about Hamida and her baby. They can be part of our family. We must help her when she comes back.'

Hamida came the night before the coaches were to take them to the boat. Her tiny daughter was strapped across her body, wrapped in an Indonesian shawl. The little one, still nameless, slept, while everyone admired her shock of black hair, her long, elegant lashes and the exquisite perfection of her tiny ears.

'See, Mahtab,' said her mother, 'they are like

shells, beautiful little shells. That's how you were when you were a baby.'

~~~

The baby slept in her mother's arms the next morning as the group assembled at the front of the hotel. Two coaches were waiting. The Egyptian man, wearing spotless white robes and wrap-around sunglasses, his gold gleaming, yelled orders and then checked names as each family came forward and placed their luggage on board.

'Will we see Dad tonight?' asked Soraya.

'Not tonight. The trip takes a few days. But we are getting closer.'

The coaches raced along the freeway.

They were headed for a port town south-east of Jakarta. They had just left the city's outskirts and were into the stretches of farmland when they heard a siren and a police van drew alongside the coach.

'*God preserve us.*' Mahtab's mother pulled her veil across her face and whispered further prayers.

After a moment, their driver stopped and then two policemen came onto the coach and spoke with the Egyptian man. He climbed down with them and Mahtab watched as he waved his hands, pointing to the coach and then in the direction that they were headed. Everyone was silent.

For fifteen minutes the argument continued.

Then the policemen turned and walked away. The Egyptian man spat on the ground and stormed back onto the coach.

He spoke to the group in Arabic, flinging the words into the air. One of the men stood next to him and translated into Dari.

'We have to go back,' he said. 'There are more police at the port and they will stop us boarding the boat. This man tells us that there is another one we can get tomorrow but we must go back to the hotel tonight.'

'Is it just money they want?' Mahtab whispered to her mother.

'I don't know.'

'Will we have rooms at the hotel again?' someone asked.

'If there is a problem, we will go somewhere else. I will find you a place to sleep. Don't worry.' The Egyptian man spoke to the driver who slowly turned the coach around and headed back the way they had come. The second coach followed.

Mahtab half closed her eyes until they were narrow slits. She slumped down low in her seat, watching the tall, sleek-looking agent with his gleaming gold, his perfect hair, his spotless robe. What did he know of hiding in trucks, of men in black turbans, of a father who left in the night and never rang?

She wanted to burst with screaming. She covered her face with her hands and turned to the wall.

~~~~~

There were rooms at the hotel but somehow the cool tiles and the soft beds felt different. Mahtab didn't want the comfort of a shower, a circling fan and a hot meal. When Farhad and Ahmad urged her to come to the recreation room and watch television, even though they didn't understand the language, she shook her head.

'Come with us then,' said her mother. She was nursing the new baby. Soraya stood on tiptoes, peering down at the sleeping girl. 'Come and I'll show you how to change her nappy.'

Mahtab shook her head again. She wandered through the corridors, her eyes down, barely lifting her feet as she walked. When she reached the verandah outside her room she flopped on the tiles and leant back against the post.

What would the story be tomorrow? Maybe that man organised it like this. He knew the police would stop them. Tomorrow he could have another reason why they couldn't go and then he would demand the very last bit of money that everyone had. And they would have to pay. They had no choice. They were on the edge of the sea in a strange country. Strangers in a strange land. Strangers for ever. So near to where their fathers were. So far from their homeland. And if they didn't have enough money?

Mahtab rolled onto her belly and stretched her hand out to the rock pool. She trailed her fingers again in the cool water. Thin weed fronds tickled her. Tiny red fish darted between the stones. She leant further forward and stared at her face in the water. Across that image floated a larger fish. Dead. Fatter than all the others, its body still, its eyes dull, lifeless.

Mahtab pulled back. *Stop thinking like this. You really are going crazy. Of course we will get a boat tomorrow. We will have enough money if he asks for more and then we will sail to Australia and Dad will be there. Dad will be there. He will.*

~~~~~

They left very early the next morning. The route they took was the same as the previous day – past the large hotels set back in lush gardens, past the suburbs with shops and houses pushing up against each other and then on to stretches of flat, open farmland. They passed through village after village where children on their way to school in shiny white-and-navy uniforms looked up at them and waved. They waved back.

They smelt the sea and the dockland before they saw it. A few hundred metres back from the water, their coach turned into a lane so narrow that other vehicles could not pass. They stepped down and around puddles of water, with slicks of gleaming oil.

The rest of the group, those who had been on the other coach, were already ahead of them, standing and squatting in front of a dilapidated wooden building about fifty metres from the water's edge.

'Is that our boat?' Farhad pointed at a small vessel pulled up at a rickety wooden pier.

'Can't be,' said Mahtab. 'It's too small.' She shielded her eyes and scanned the horizon.

It was as she had never seen it before. A straight line. No, a line that curved slightly down at each end. Blue met blue. Or was it green? The sea. The sky. It really was like glass. She breathed deeply, feeling the salt air go into her nostrils and dance its way down her throat. Her lungs filled and she knew she was smiling. There was a larger boat out there, she could see it now. It beckoned her with every dip and bob on the shifting, shimmering water. Beyond that: maybe Dad.

~~~

The Egyptian man had disappeared into the shed and he came out now with an Indonesian man who set up a table and a chair. He announced to the group that they would use the smaller boat to go out to the larger one, that this process would take about an hour and that then they would be leaving and heading for the port of Darwin, the northernmost city in Australia.

Mahtab still stared at the sea. She looked up as birds shrieked above them and then darted down into the water. One disappeared then rose skyward again, a struggling silver fish in its beak. She left the others and walked down to where small waves nibbled at the sand. She squatted and stretched out her hand and let the water run over it. The sun glinted off her golden bracelet. Tiny white bubbles of foam clung to her skin for a moment and then were gone. Mahtab laughed and pushed her fingers into the yielding sand. She found a shell, a small one with a smooth underside although the outer edge was ribbed and bumpy. She rinsed it. It was like the tiny ear of some creature that lived in the depths of the sea. Where had it come from? Had it started somewhere else and been brought by the sea, carried on these curling waves? She tucked it into her pocket and looked back to where her mother stood talking to the man at the table.

Hamida was there. Farhad, Ahmad and Soraya too. They beckoned to Mahtab.

'What is it? What's the matter?'

'Money. They want more money for the baby.'

'That's stupid. She doesn't take up any room.'

'It doesn't matter. They can ask for whatever they want.'

'Well, give it to them.'

Her mother shook her head. 'Hamida doesn't have enough money left.'

'What will they do? They can't leave her behind?'

'That's what they are saying.'

'Do we have much left?'

'There is a little. I spent most of it on food for the next few days.'

The motor boat carrying the first load of people for the fishing boat started up. People jostled forward like birds squabbling for a food scrap.

'Give her our money, Mum. Dad will meet us and he will have more.' Farhad looked serious.

Mahtab's mother hesitated. 'It's not that simple.'

The man at the table tapped his pencil. Hamida's shoulders dropped. Mahtab's mother put her arm around the younger woman and spoke quickly. The expression on the face of the man at the table didn't change.

Mahtab reached inside her sleeve and felt the coins that hung from the chain around her wrist. Grandma's chain. Could she?

A squawking bird landed at her feet. It pushed its red beak hard into the sand, then rose triumphant, a small creature dangling from its mouth.

Mahtab slid the bracelet into her hand. Her wrist felt cold, bare. She ran her thumb over the rough edges of the coins.

'Give them this, Mum.'

'No, Mahtab. That is yours. It is not to be used.'

'Do you have any other idea? You said they are

family now.' She pressed the bracelet into her mother's hand. 'Grandma would understand.'

Her mother lifted her daughter's hands to her lips. 'You are a girl to be proud of. I will buy you another in Australia. With the first money we have.'

Mahtab turned away. She tasted salt on her lips – sea spray or tears? She wasn't sure.

~~~~~

There were so many people on the small boat that they had to stand, clinging to each other as it pushed through the water. Mahtab didn't care. She stood, wedged against the outer rail, feeling the salt spray on her face, her hands and her bare lower arms. She breathed in the diesel and stared at the horizon. Somewhere out there, over that edge of the sea, was Australia. *We are coming. We are coming.*

It was hard pulling themselves up onto the fishing boat. First the luggage went and then the children, almost passed hand over hand. Hamida kept the baby bound tightly to her chest. Then it was Mahtab's turn. She pushed the fisherman's hand away and gripped the metal rungs. The ladder bounced and crashed against the boat as she climbed, but she hung on and reached the top with only a bruise to her knee.

There was barely enough room. Men and the bigger boys gathered in groups on the deck. They made positions for themselves, marking off areas with their boxes and bags. Almost all the women and children had gone down below. A crewman pointed to the steps going down into the belly of the boat.

'No, Farhad.' Their mother called the boy back. 'No. We are not going down there.' She pulled Farhad, Soraya and Mahtab to her. 'We are staying up here with Hamida and Ahmad.' She pushed past the sailor and forced her way to a position on the far side of the deck. 'I think this is a big mistake,' she whispered to Mahtab. 'This boat is too small and too flimsy. Look at that.' She pointed to the rotting wooden frame that made a small shelter for the man who held the wheel. 'They told me we were getting a fine steel boat with special equipment for storms.' She stamped her foot and left an indent on the decking. 'If it's as rotten down underneath as it is on the top we'll all end up at the bottom of the sea.'

Mahtab saw the chipped and flaking timber. Paint had peeled from it long ago and there was glass in only one of the window frames of the tiny room around the wheel. Truly what the man had said and what they now sailed on were as alike as a fish and a bird. She pushed from her mind her thoughts that anything else he said might also be untrue.

'I think we should leave, right now,' said her mother. 'I haven't brought you so far to end up dead at sea. I don't trust this.'

'No.' Farhad sat down at her feet. 'We have to stay on board. You said I could be Sinbad.'

'Hmm, we all know what happened to him,' said his mother.

They heard raised voices then. The Iraqi men at the front of the boat were yelling at a crewman. They waved their arms and made punching gestures into their fists. The sailor was much smaller than them and he drew back until another man who Mahtab decided was the captain came forward. He spoke just as angrily as his passengers and they shrugged then and turned away and sat down on the deck.

'It'll be all right, Mum,' said Mahtab. 'They wouldn't sail this boat if it wasn't strong enough. We have to stay on board. It's the only way we'll get to Dad. He's waiting for us.'

Her mother pulled her burqa around her and sat down with her back to the wheelhouse. Hamida joined her and the younger children too found a place near them. Only Mahtab stayed standing, her damp clothes stuck to her body. She leant against the rail as she had on the smaller boat. She lifted her face to the wind and thought of the ride into Quetta. She stared down at the water and imagined the sandy bottom, the shells, the fish of all the shapes and sizes she had ever seen in the market. And would there be a whale? She turned to the horizon and pushed from her mind any thought that her father would not be there to meet them.

Chapter Eight

THE ENGINE OF the boat started and Mahtab felt the movement change. They were no longer moving up and down with a gentle rhythm but were heading away from the land and the smaller boat. The man from Egypt stood in that one, his hand raised in a wave to them all. Long after they could no longer see the boat, his white robe was still visible against the darkness of the land.

For about half an hour, Mahtab stood there, staring at the water and the sea ahead of her. The hot sun had dried her clothes in minutes. Gradually, she realised that she was thirsty. She joined her mother and the others and shared some bread and a mug of water.

'Tell us about Sinbad, Mum,' said Farhad. 'Tell me about me.'

So their mother told them one of the stories of the great Sinbad who sought his fortune on the sea. She chose the one when Sinbad set out from his home in Baghdad with lots of things to trade with other countries. 'The voyage was good,' she said, 'until one day the captain landed his boat on an island and the crew and the passengers were relaxing and enjoying the break from the harsher life at sea. Suddenly that island moved and the captain called to everyone that this was not an island at all where he had landed. It was the back of a whale. They were terrified. They raced to the boat and cast off. Sinbad didn't make it. He was further from what he thought was the beach and so when he reached the water he saw his ship moving away from him as fast as its sails would take it. All his money and his goods were on that ship. Poor Sinbad. After that he was thrown into the water and he thought he would drown, but he didn't. He was washed up on a real island where he had lots and lots of different adventures.'

'Will that happen to me?' Farhad's eyes were large.

His mother reached out and drew him close to her.

'No, my Sinbad. You won't fall off a whale. That's just the story.'

'What about the adventure?'

'I think,' said Mahtab, 'that what will happen to you, as it did to Sinbad, is that you'll grow rich and marry a beautiful girl. What do you think?'

'Yuk. I'll be rich but I'm not marrying anybody.'

The stories went on till it was almost night. On the lower deck someone was cooking fish and the smell of that mixed with the diesel fumes drifted up and over the family.

'I'm hungry,' said Soraya. 'Have we got some kebab?'

Their mother shook her head. She passed them more bread and cold cooked vegetables, nuts and dried fruit. 'This will be fine for us for a few days,' she said. 'We'll be in Australia by then.'

They slept, wrapped around each other against the chill of the breeze off the water, like puppies in a box of straw. Some time in the night Mahtab woke. Hamida was rocking her baby, softly singing to it the same words Mahtab remembered her mother singing in the truck so many weeks ago.

La la la la sleep,
Because the night is long,
It's too early for you to count the stars yet,
Some people are smiling even in their dreams,
Some people have wet eyes even in their sleep,
La la la la sleep.

Mahtab rolled over and looked up at the stars. The night was clear. There was a full moon and that scattering of diamonds again. She hadn't looked, not properly, since that icy cold night in the mountains. So long ago.

She tried to find the stars that she knew, but there were so many, and she was confused. Some looked like Castor, Pollux and the Great Bear but they weren't where she remembered them, so she wasn't sure. She tried to imagine the different clusters as animal shapes from pictures she had seen in books a long time ago.

The next night was the same. The boat rocked gently, someone was singing and Mahtab lay staring upwards. Maybe these were the stars that looked down on Australia. Maybe they were different because it was a different land. She tried to imagine the country and how her life would be. Uncle Karim had sent a storybook from Paris and the children in the pictures had golden hair and rosy cheeks and they wore short dresses that showed their knees and they had kittens and little dogs that licked their hands and faces. The same children were in the television show that came from America. She could remember from before the time when the televisions were thrown into the street and their own set had been hidden away and only turned on when it was safe to do so. Shiny-topped kitchen benches, smiling mothers. Would Mum smile again in Australia?

~~~

On the fourth day they woke early. The sun was not yet up but streaks of light caught the edges of the cloud that had gathered above them in the night. A strong wind blew on their faces, not cold but salt-laden and drying. Mahtab pulled the end of her veil across her mouth. The boat rocked, more strongly than before. Boxes slid along the deck.

'It's like the swing at home.' Farhad clapped but Mahtab saw the look in her mother's eye and held on tightly to his waist.

All morning they rode the waves like wild camels. First one way, then another, the wind and the water conspired like angry herdsmen determined to break the animals' spirit. They gripped hold of each other, the children sheltered in the centre of their group. Mahtab clung to her mother on one side and Hamida on the other. Sea spray soaked them and all their possessions. Food and utensils, clothing and sheets of paper flew past them and into the water. Hour after hour. The clouds grew black. Over the sound of the roaring sea came rumblings of thunder and fearsome slashes of lightning. Again and again white light broke the darkness. And then the rain started.

Rain.

Rain.

Rain.

Buckets of hard, driving water pounded their heads, their shoulders and their bodies. Like stones hurled from the sky, the rain struck and then bounced to the deck. They could not speak for the lashing, screaming sound and the effort needed to hold onto each other. Soraya's arms were wrapped tightly around Mahtab's legs, her face pressed almost to the ground.

Then the rain came sideways, blasting into them, sending sheets of water across the deck, into the wheelhouse, pushing all before it. Heads tucked down, bodies braced against the wall of water, they endured. Again and again, the boat heaved and stretched. The sea was tall mountains and deep valleys and they were tossed from crest to crest as it raged and boiled beneath them.

Mahtab tried to count backwards. It didn't work. It needed a calmer, focused mind. Each time she started, a sudden different twist of the boat or blast of water jolted her into grasping more tightly, straining to cling to those who held on with her.

Clothes soaked and clinging to her skin, her veil blown from her head so that her wild, wet hair blew across her face, Mahtab tried to pray. *Allah, deliver me from this and I will be the best daughter anyone could be. Save me from this and I will say my prayers diligently, learn the Koran off by heart, do everything that you or my parents and my teachers ask of me. I will work hard and I will give my money to the mosque. I will be the best person. Save us all, please, please, please.*

For hours it went on. Mahtab's body ached from the effort of bracing herself against the wind. And then, when she was shivering, taut, numb with the wet and the cold, the storm died. As quickly as it had arisen, it dropped away. They loosened their hold on each other and collapsed onto the deck. 'We are alive. Thank God we are alive,' whispered Mahtab's mother. The colour was gone from her face; her lips were cracked and bleeding.

Mahtab's hands were white, fixed into frozen, claw-like shapes. She blew on them, sucked them and rubbed and rubbed them until she could feel again.

Sailors rushed up and down the steps to the lower part of the boat, buckets in hand. Mahtab stretched and stood up as a woman came up from below, wet clothes plastered to her body.

'We're sinking,' she said. 'Water is coming in.'

The captain passed them, touching each of the men, urging them to come with him. Long into the night the bucket brigade worked. Sailors and passengers alike formed queues that passed the buckets down empty and then took them, slopping water underfoot as they came up full.

Mahtab was still as wet as if she had been dropped in a tub of water. She joined her mother in wringing out whatever clothes could be taken off and searching for their food. They found only sodden breads and a few handfuls of nuts and soggy fruit. Hamida rubbed the limbs of her tiny baby, trying to get her warm. Mahtab watched, her eyes drooping until, still cold and wet, she fell asleep against her mother, under a starless sky.

~~~~~

The next day there was no sun. Everyone watched the sky, waiting, fearful of rain that did not come. The boat rolled and Mahtab felt the contents of her stomach shift and rise. For a moment she thought she was going to be sick and she moved to the edge of the boat. Soraya joined her there. 'Will Dad meet us?' she said.

'Of course.'

'Are you sure?'

'I told you. He rang.' Mahtab could not look at her sister. What would she say when she found out the lie? What would Mum say?

'But will he know me?'

'What do you mean?'

'My hair is longer and now I am six. I was five when he last saw me.'

'He'll know you,' said Mahtab. 'Your face is so familiar to him from all the years when he played with you in the garden and when he told you stories. He could never, ever forget you.'

'But I think I am forgetting him,' said Soraya, and her lips trembled.

Mahtab reached out and pulled her sister to her. 'That's because you're little. Your memory hasn't had lots of practice. When you see him, you'll know him. Let's sit down and see what we remember together.'

~~~

Later in the day she was sick. The boat rocked and the smell of diesel brought the contents of her stomach, the small handful of nuts and bread, to her mouth. She made it to the side again and clung to the rail, trembling. Farhad lay listless at their mother's feet. Ahmad too. The baby in Hamida's lap whimpered.

'It is time we named this child,' she said to Mahtab's mother. 'But I haven't the heart. I cannot think of her name while everything is so unknown.'

'In Australia, when we land. That will be soon enough.'

~~~

Mahtab knew there was little food left. She didn't care. She couldn't eat. But she was thirsty. Her skin was burnt, her nose peeling, her lips cracked and dry. She heard loud voices from the front of the boat. A woman was cursing her husband, who had taken the water she was saving for her children. Mahtab watched as the man struck his wife hard across the face. She fell back, nursing her cheek.

Her father would never strike her mother. He would give his last drop of water to his children.

~~~

The bucket brigade continued. For a second night, the men pounded the steps, up and back, up and back. Did they sleep? Would they stop? If they did, would the boat sink? Was Mum right? Should they have stayed in Indonesia? Should they have waited for another boat? Would there have been another boat? Mahtab's legs were stiff and her stomach was a tight, hard knot. Why was it this way? Why?

A loud scream. The loudest, ever. A ship. There was a ship and it was coming towards them. Women cheered. Men clapped and fell to the deck giving thanks. Farhad lifted his head and then pushed himself up.

'We are saved,' said their mother. 'Thanks be to God. It's a big, big ship.'

'Has it come from Australia?' Soraya stood on her toes trying to see beyond the mass of bodies.

'It must be,' said Mahtab. 'Maybe it's a special ship from Australia and it's come to welcome us.'

But there was no welcome. As their boat drew closer to the huge steel vessel, a voice came over a loudhailer. It was in a language Mahtab had never heard before. The whole boat grew silent. Then there was a murmur. Someone knew the words, translated them first into Arabic, then Dari. The murmur grew. Louder and louder.

'They say we are not welcome.'

'We must go back.'

'Turn around.'

'Return.'

'We can't.'

'Cannot.'

'We will die.'

'Die.'

'No.'

'No!'

'NO!'

Such sound coming from Mahtab's mother. She stood on the deck, her burqa fallen to her shoulders, her loose hair streaming behind her. Her hands were raised and her mouth opened wide, teeth bared. Cries of deep pain came from within her.

Wailing. Stamping. Crying. Hands pressed to faces. Men knelt on the deck, tore open their shirts, beat their chests, crying out that they would kill themselves there rather than be forced to return.

Mahtab didn't know where to look, couldn't believe what she heard. How could this be? Didn't they know what had happened? Didn't they know about the whips, the dogs, the beatings, shootings, stonings? The trip through the mountains? The hiding in the truck? The months, the months with no father? The tears? The tears?

Her mother dropped, curled on the deck, her head on her knees, her arms wrapping her robe tightly around them. She rocked and rocked, a thin, plaintive howl coming from somewhere deep inside her. Soraya and Farhad knelt, stroking her, patting her. Hamida sat there too, staring, her baby screaming in her lap.

The boat turned around, westward. The captain put a sailor at the wheel and went to talk with the Iraqi men. Then the word came down, from one person to another, one language to another. We are not going back. We will not return. When it's dark we try again. They waited, the engine barely ticking over. The huge steel ship seemed to stay still, watching them, and then it turned to the south and slowly, slowly moved away.

Mahtab stared after it until it disappeared. Ahead of them, the sun was low. She gazed at it, silent. She saw the lower edge of it touch the place where sky and water met. Slowly but definitely the whole ball of it dipped. Half was in view, then a quarter, then a fine sliver and it was gone. The sky glowed red and gold. That too gradually faded. Mahtab felt the engine beneath her kick and charge and then the small boat gradually turned to the north. It was moving faster than at any time in the voyage. It turned again. The place where the sun had gone was now behind them. There was a hush. The normally noisy children sat quiet now as their parents scanned the horizon. Some looked back, daring that huge ship to return, while others looked forward, willing land to come into view.

~~~

All night they sailed. Some slept fitfully. Others sat, all night, staring out ahead. The family barely spoke. They were so near. So near. As dawn broke, a cry rang out. Ships. Boats. They did not leap to their feet and rush to the side this time. Nervous, bitten, they waited. A smaller steel boat this time came closer and closer. Again the loud voices were hurled across the water. This time the captain stayed at the wheel. The murmur started, rose to shouting.

'We are going to Darwin.'

'We are to go ahead.'

'They are following us in.'

'We are safe.'

'Safe.'

Young men danced on the foredeck. Prayers were said. Tears, this time of joy, flowed. Mahtab hugged her mother. Soraya and Farhad, seasickness and sunburn forgotten, flung their arms around each other and danced. Hamida smiled for the first time and embraced everyone, passing the baby from one to the other. The little one gripped Mahtab's finger and Mahtab bent forward and kissed her face, fiercely.

They saw land. Ships' masts, tall buildings, headlands, trees. Gradually Australia became real. Like sheep before the herdsman's dog, they went before the ship into the harbour of Darwin.

Sea birds soared above them, squawking, wheeling and diving. Everyone rushed to the front of the boat. Mahtab tried to see between the bodies, tried to stand on tiptoe, on boxes to see over them. She could not believe this feeling. Her tired eyes, tired body, tired mind drank in everything before her. Sheds and cranes and boxes as big as houses. Trees of all sizes. Green. Green. Green. People everywhere, their arms showing, their faces naked. No beards. Would her father too have no beard?

She wanted to leap from her place. She knew he could not be there but she wanted to hurl herself down the gangplank and land on the shore, searching the faces of men for him. This was as he had promised. She was a bird, ready to soar and swoop: free. Free. FREE.

Chapter Nine

NO DAD.

Of course he wasn't there.

No leaping from the deck onto the land. No running down the gangway, smiling, welcomed. Official men in short trousers, their legs hairy for all to see, came on board and strode up and down, searching for someone who could understand their language. Mahtab turned her back on them and gathered up the family's bags. The officials spoke to the captain in rough voices and then they took him away and the other Indonesian men too.

'We are to line up,' came the murmur, 'with our papers.'

But their papers were gone.

'We are no longer Turkish holiday-makers,' Mahtab's mother had said when first they came on board the boat. She had torn the documents to shreds and held them out, letting the wind snatch them and blow them high into the air.

They were not alone. Family after family shrugged their shoulders and shook their heads when asked for passports, identity cards, anything that could tell the authorities who they truly were.

The men in uniform, now joined by women with hard faces, gathered in small groups and hissed. Their tight shoulders told their anger. They turned back and spoke roughly and pushed the men into lines.

Everyone straggled down onto the wharf. No one met them. More herding, this time to a huge galvanised-iron shed. A wall of heat. They dropped their luggage and slumped to the floor as the men were taken to the far end of the building. More men in uniforms sat at wide tables.

'What's happening?' said Soraya. 'Where's Dad? I want my dad. You said he told us to come. You said he would be here.'

'He doesn't know that we were on that boat,' said Mahtab. 'He is here. He is in this country but maybe he thought we would come to land in a different place.' The words tumbled out freely. Did she believe it herself? Would she keep saying these things to Soraya for ever? How easy it was to lie.

'I'm thirsty,' said Farhad.

'Sshh. We're all thirsty,' said Mahtab.

'And I'm hot.' Soraya lay, limp against her sister's leg.

Mahtab didn't have the energy to add that they were all hot. She fanned her face with the end of her veil and watched as the uniformed women came then and gestured for the mothers to go with them for questioning. Soraya, Farhad and Ahmad clung to Mahtab as their mothers moved down the long building.

'They won't be long,' Mahtab heard herself whispering and didn't know why.

~~~~

After a long time water was brought to them, and soft bread with slices of cold meat and pale yellow cheese. Farhad wrinkled his nose, but they all ate and then the men and women came back. No one knew exactly what was to happen.

The sky grew dark. A rumble of thunder shook the shed. Lightning crackled and then rain came. Loud, driving rain pelting the tin roof like gunfire. Through the opening they saw people running the length of the wharf, newspapers or jackets over their heads.

And then it stopped. A bus drew up at the entrance to the shed. It was so like the coach they had ridden to the boat five days before that Mahtab thought it would take them back to the harbour. Were they being sent back to Indonesia?

'I don't want to go,' she said. 'They can't send us back.'

'We are not going back.' Her mother handed her a bag to carry. 'There are laws to protect us in this country. We are safe here. We are probably going to a hotel.'

~~~

They drove through the city streets. Like Indonesia, this place was green. Huge houses, large enough for families of many children, were set back in gardens, planted with the same intense flowers as their hotel in Jakarta. The roofs were like triangles, like pictures Mahtab had seen in storybooks. No one could sleep on them when the night was hot.

Then they went past shops. Bread and pastries, cakes with icing of different bright colours, meat hanging in the windows, sausages, chickens and whole sides of beef. It was like a market turned outwards. Then clothing, long elegant dresses that Mahtab had only seen in pictures, trousers and shirts, splashes of colour, glimpsed then gone. Cars everywhere. People hurried along the brick-paved

121

footpath or leant against posts and the walls of buildings. Many had skin that was black or darker brown than Mahtab had ever seen. Some were almost naked. Arms and legs uncovered. No burqas, no veils, not even a scarf. There were men with no shirt on and she turned away from the sight of the hair on their backs, their arms and their chests. The coach stopped at a traffic light. Three girls about Mahtab's size were standing by a yellow post. They wore tiny tops, held up by thin straps over their pink shoulders. Their light brown hair hung loose. One sucked on a green icecream. She saw Mahtab staring at her and she took the icecream away from her face and poked her tongue out. It was green too. She pointed, laughing, until Mahtab looked away.

Stranger in a strange land. This is not my place. These are not my people. She tried to push it from her mind, to concentrate on what was before her: an open space, full of cars, and in the centre of it, a tree. A fat, squat tree, its trunk swollen at the base and for the first few metres of its trunk. It was a round old man, dug in, unmovable, like a picture of the Buddha she had seen once but she couldn't remember where. A black-and-white dog lay in the thin sliver of shade, its tail lifting lazily and then falling back.

If they were going to a hotel, it was a long way from the centre of town. Mahtab grew more and more sleepy as they passed through street after street of houses. They were smaller than the ones near the harbour and then there were blocks of land with no houses at all, just shimmering stretches of long grass.

The bus was cool and the road was smooth but her body still felt as it had when she was on the sea and it seemed to rock as if the road was the gentlest of waves.

~~~

Mahtab woke with the sun burning her face. The green had gone. The land was now so brown that for a moment she was home again in Afghanistan, staring out at the dry earth. But the brown was different, redder, and the trees were wrong too. And there were no mountains. Everywhere, as far as she could see, it was flat. Flat, flat, flat.

Farhad woke too and pressed his nose against the glass. 'Where are we? Where are we going?'

They drove for hours and hours. Fruit was passed around, and water bottles. The view from the window never changed.

Some of the men grew angry. One strode up and down the aisle of the coach, shouting that they were not being treated well and wanting to know where they were going. He urged the others to join his protest. A uniformed woman met him in the aisle and yelled at him until he sat down, red-faced, his shoulders hunched.

~~~

Mahtab supposed they were headed to another town – maybe the hotels in the other place were full – but they passed through towns, two or three of them, and didn't stop. She drifted in and out of sleep. She felt so glad to be off that boat, to be on land, but why must they keep travelling? Somewhere they must stop. She closed her eyes and tried to imagine her father's face, nothing but that.

How he would smile and laugh to see them. How he would wrap his arms around them and plant kisses on their faces. He would throw Soraya into the air and find words, names he had used for them when they were babies. But if…?

Across the aisle from her, she saw that her mother slept, and Soraya too.

Night turned to day, then night again and another day.

At last they turned off the road and drove along a narrower strip of bitumen. This time there were no trees on either side. Mahtab could hear murmurings up the front of the bus, angry voices in a language that was not her own. The voices grew louder and then she too saw what was ahead of them.

Long rows of buildings, four or five of them, and

around them a fence, steel mesh with barbed wire on the top and the sun glinting off it enough to make you shield your eyes. The murmuring stopped. And then 'This is a prison,' came a voice from the back of the bus.

Another joined in. 'We have done nothing.'

'We are refugees, we have escaped Saddam.'

'We have fled the Taliban.'

'They said this is a free country.'

'Why do you do this to us?'

'Why?'

'Why?'

'Why?'

Mahtab looked across to her mother. Her face was grey and she clutched Soraya's hand and her lips were pressed tight together. She was wrapped up in sadness and Mahtab knew she had no answers to such questions. There were none to give.

~~~

Everyone climbed down, sullen, wary. They stood with their backs to the coach, facing more men and women in uniform – prison guards with two-way radios clipped to their pockets, batons hanging from their belts. Farhad and Soraya hid behind their mother but Mahtab took a deep breath and stepped up beside her, trying to look as tall as she could. She shielded her eyes from the glare. Her heart was fluttering like a caged bird again.

A skinny pink guard with pale ginger hair and a floppy moustache stood in front of them and held out a sheet of paper. He called out names, barely recognisable in his strange voice, and then other words. When Mahtab's mother stepped forward, the woman guard beside him pointed to a building and said the words again. They didn't understand but crossed the yard behind her, went through a wire fence and gate and climbed the wooden steps to their new home.

It was bare, just beds and a rail to hang clothes on, a tiny cupboard, a shelf and a chair. There was a window too, open, but it had bars. Mahtab gripped them and pressed her nose between them. Beyond, she saw more treeless yard, another high fence, and then long rows of other buildings. People were sitting around in small groups, children were playing in the dust and all around were more wire fences, holding them in. She laughed. Why bar the window when they were held in by that wire fence? And a world of flat, brown land beyond that.

Mum closed the door.

'Where is my father?' Soraya tugged at Mum's robe. 'Mahtab said he would meet us. Why are we here?'

Mahtab looked away.

Mum sat on the bed and kicked off her dusty sandals.

'I don't know. I don't know where he is and I don't know how long we will be here. What I do know is what your father told me. This is a free country and they will treat us with justice, according to the law. You must stay strong and ready to meet your father as soon as he comes for us or we can go to him.' She bent down and opened her bag. She took out the small jar of earth that Mahtab had not seen since the day they sat on the mountain, looking down over the valley. 'This is going to be our home for a while. I don't know how long. But while we are here, this will remind us of where we have come from, who we are.' She placed the small jar against her lips and put it on the shelf. Mahtab tried to remember the moment when that jar was filled. They had been high in the mountains, on the side of the road. It had been cold. There had been snow. She could not, in this heat, bring to her body the sensation of snow.

~~~

Mahtab was hollow. Empty, as if her flesh and blood, her energy that kept her breathing and running, thinking and talking, was gone. Nothing was in its place. She was hungry for food but she knew that she would bring it back up. Not because she was on a small boat, rocking on the rough sea of a broad ocean,

127

but because the will to hold it inside her was gone. She was hungry. Hungry for water, for her father, for her grandmother, her aunts and uncles, for the trees in the back yard, the cabinet against the wall, the silver and glass objects so lovingly collected, for her mountains, the jagged peaks that cut the sky.

Her father was dead. She felt sure of it. She was just a speck of dirt on the floor, drifting through the gap between the boards, falling to the ground.

~~~

That night, Farhad and Mahtab each took the narrow beds and Soraya crept in beside their mother on the larger one. Mahtab lay in the darkness, listening. It felt strange to be lying still, no rocking boat, no crowded bodies pressing up against her, no smells of other people. No coach rolling along a highway. She stretched out under the cool sheet. Maybe she was wrong. Maybe things would be all right. Maybe Dad wasn't dead. He would find them here. He would come and sign some papers or pay some money and they would go with him and stay with him, somewhere. She would have a room again with her things, a bed with a cover she had chosen herself and a soft, soft pillow to bury her hair in. Voices murmured from outside or the next room. Then silence. She slept.

Heavy boots sounded outside their door. Mahtab grabbed the edge of the sheet and pulled it tightly around her, up to her eyes. She couldn't breathe. The door opened and torchlight shone on her face. It flicked around the room, resting for a moment on Farhad, on Soraya and on her mother. Something was said in English. She shivered but she wasn't cold. The door closed.

Mum said nothing but Mahtab knew from her breathing that she wasn't asleep. Soraya made some little noise and Mum started to sing then, softly, that old song from the truck, the one that Hamida had sung on the boat.

La la la la sleep,
Because the night is long,
It's too early for you to count the stars yet,
Some people are smiling even in their dreams,
Some people have wet eyes even in their sleep,
La la la la sleep.

Chapter Ten

A BELL WOKE them. A shrill, raucous sound, drilling its way into their heads.

'What do we do?' Farhad stood in the middle of the room, his clothes rumpled, his hair sticking up like grass after a windstorm.

'We get dressed neatly and then we go to wash and we find out what we are to do.' Their mother's voice was firm but there were dark bags under her eyes.

They came out of their room and saw those who had arrived on the coaches with them walking towards a separate green building. They fell in behind Hamida, carrying her baby, Ahmad grabbing at her legs.

Beyond the fences they could see more buildings and people.

'Why are we here and they there?' said Mahtab.

'I don't know.' Her mother led them to the queue, waiting to enter the green building. They were served a plate of chicken and rice and sat down at a long table. Mum and Hamida talked in soft voices. Mahtab stirred her food and looked around to see if there were any other girls her age. How long since she had thought of Leila. Where was she now? Was she in prison too?

Table after table was filled by men with occasionally one or two women and their children. Some men were like her dad with dark hair and beard. Some men were black. One or two had their young children with them but most were alone.

After breakfast, they went back to the room to wash, and their mother told them that she had some news of what would happen.

'We will be interviewed,' she said. 'Hamida spoke with a nurse who came to check the baby. She says they will ask us about why we came here to Australia and why we have no papers. I will ask them to help us to find your father. I will tell them of the things that were happening to our family, what happened to your grandfather, and then I know they will tell us that we can stay.'

'Here? In this prison?'

'No. No, this is just while they check us to find out who we are exactly and to make sure that we are not some dangerous person who wishes to bring harm to this country. Then we move next door, to the bigger camp, where we saw those people this morning and then, when they find your father, we can join him.'

'Then what happens? Where will we go?'

'I'm not sure. Your father told me about big cities where he would be able to work and you children would go to school and you would grow up free.'

Free? Free was how she felt when the boat came into the harbour and she touched land again. Would that feeling ever return? Mahtab dropped her veil and began to brush her hair. It was long now, way past her shoulders, and it was hard to pull the brush through the thickness of it. The scratches and sunburn on her fingers ached. Mahtab looked out through the doorway, across the bare brown earth, through the wire fence and then over more flat, brown land. She closed her eyes and tried to remember what they had seen in the city, Darwin, such a short time ago. Green gardens and green beside the road, trees along the edge of the streets and buildings that looked so new, so shiny, some as tall as any in Herat. The shops, the cars, the naked arms. Would they live in a place like that? Would they too have a garden again, fruit trees, a swing, a paddling pool for Soraya, a room of her own?

~~~~

On that first day Mahtab's mother washed and washed her hands and face. The dust of the road and the salt from the sea had worked their way into every scratch and tear in her skin. Her burqa was sun-bleached but clean, her feet brown from sun and dust. She didn't know when she would be called.

Mahtab sat with Soraya, on the step closest to their door.

Men squatted in groups, talking quietly. Guards lounged on white plastic chairs, soaking up the sun. A young woman, her head covered in a short black veil, walked the length of the perimeter fence and when she reached one end she turned and walked back again. Sometimes she stopped and held her arms high and wide, making a strange shape against the sunlight. She carried a stick that clicked softly as she ran it against the wire. Up and back. And again. And again.

Farhad and Ahmad found a friend, Hussein, from Iraq. They couldn't speak the same language but they too found sticks and started drawing in the dust. First they drew a big ship and all three stood on it and rocked and swayed but they tired of that and with their sticks behind them they rushed in wide circles, creating swirling, crazy patterns that sometimes overlapped and sometimes went off in wild designs.

And they laughed. Mahtab hadn't heard such a sound for a long time, and she found herself smiling. She knew her mother felt better for it too because she came and stood on the step and she smiled and clapped her hands at their antics. Mahtab looked again to see if there might be a friend for her, but she saw no one her age.

The interview didn't happen that day. They waited and waited and when Mahtab asked why no one came to talk to her or to send for her, her mother shrugged. 'Many people arrived yesterday, Mahtab. Why should we be the first? It may take days.'

~~~

It did.

Each morning they had their breakfast, washed and readied themselves to be called and to answer why they had left their country. For a whole week, they waited. They listened to the stories of others who had come the way they had. Some would not speak when Mahtab's mother asked them about the meeting. Others said there were too many questions and there was no way they could answer them all. One woman said that the man who translated her answers did so wrongly, she knew it from the look on his face but she didn't know the words to say it so the man in uniform would know the truth. The Iraqi woman, the one who had wanted to save the water for her children, cried.

Mahtab sat, shielding her eyes from the sun, watching the girl at the wire.

~~~~~

One morning, a young woman approached Mahtab's mother. She was the nurse who had spoken with Hamida and she did not wear the same uniform as the guards. She smiled and held out some brightly coloured books, saying words that none of them could understand.

Then she turned and said slowly, 'Cath-er-ine.'

Mahtab didn't know what to say. She looked down at her dusty feet.

The woman reached forward and took her hand. She pointed to herself. 'Cath-er-ine,' she said again. She pointed to Mahtab and raised her eyebrows.

Mahtab didn't answer.

'Cath-er-ine,' the woman said again.

'Mah-tab,' Mahtab whispered.

'Mah-tab. My name is Mahtab,' said Catherine, each word coming from her as a slow, distinct and rounded sound.

'My – name – is – Mah-tab.' Slowly the sounds came, louder now.

Catherine smiled and said something that

135

Mahtab didn't understand. She pushed the books into Mahtab's mother's hand.

'My – name – is – Mah-tab,' said Mahtab to her mother. 'My – name – is – Mah-tab,' as she stood beneath the shower, as she brushed her hair at night, as she lay in her bed, waiting for sleep to come.

Catherine came a second time. She sat, repeating the phrases, smiling at Mahtab.

My name is Mahtab.

I am from Afghanistan.

I am twelve years old.

How are you?

I am well, thank you.

Gradually the writing in the book began to make sense. Sometimes Catherine came to where Mahtab and her mother sat on the steps of their building and she would point to the words beneath the pictures on the page. 'Bus. Tram. Train. Ship.' They repeated the words slowly. 'Bread. Rice. Carrot. Potato.' Sometimes it seemed to Mahtab that the words came out like the strangled sounds of a fighting cat. Catherine laughed and they laughed with her.

~~~

During that time, the interview happened. Mahtab wanted to go with her mother, to ask why they were in prison like this, like common criminals, when they had done nothing wrong. But when she went with her mother to the main building, the pink-and-ginger man told her to go back to their section.

She sat in the doorway watching Farhad, Ahmad and Hussein. They had some words now, or at least they spoke to each other in their own languages, but whether they understood, she couldn't tell. Soraya climbed on her lap. 'Tell me the kangaroo story.' She pushed her head into Mahtab's shoulder.

'No.'

'Please.'

'I don't feel like it.'

'Please, please.'

'Oh, all right.' Mahtab told her again the story of the father who buys the pet kangaroo for his little girl. She wondered, as she spoke, if their own father was alive or dead, if such a creature did exist, or if it was all a fantasy from the storybook he had read. Maybe nothing he had told her then was true. Or had he arrived like they had? Was he too locked up behind some barbed and cruel wire?

Their mother came back. Mahtab couldn't tell from her face what the meeting had been like. She went straight into the room and she sat on the bed and Mahtab followed to sit at her feet.

'What did they say?'

She shook her head.

'Tell me, Mum. What did they say? Why are we here? Can we leave now?'

She reached down and stroked Mahtab's hair. 'Sshh, little one. They say we are illegal. Queue-jumpers.' She laughed, bitterly. 'As if there was a queue for us. We have broken the law by coming the way we did. We must wait while all our documents are checked and our situation is examined, and they said that can take a long time, maybe years.' Mahtab heard the tremble in her voice.

'It could take years, and sometimes...' She stopped whatever it was she was going to say.

'Sometimes what?'

'You don't want to know, darling. You don't want to know.'

'I do. I am old enough to be told. I am old enough to hide silent in a truck as it goes through the mountains, as it was crawled over by Taliban, to stand with you in airports and on the deck of a ship. I haven't cried out or betrayed us. I am old enough to know.'

'Sometimes people are sent back to the country they came from.'

Her words were a kick in Mahtab's stomach. A heavy boot that sent the air gasping from her throat. Go back! Back to the black turbans and the whips and the cries of the women and fear, the cold, cold fear that one day there would be that knock on the door.

No, Mahtab wanted to scream, *No No No*, but the trapdoor had dropped, shutting her throat, and she flung herself on the bed in silence.

The two young children were already asleep when Mahtab and her mother prepared for bed. 'You sleep with Soraya,' said Mum and she took Mahtab's mattress and pushed it on the floor across the doorway.

'To protect you all,' she said simply. 'To make sure no one comes in here at night, to get at any of you.'

'But who would want to come in here?' Mahtab said.

'It has happened. One of the women told me. You're too young to worry about things like this. Let me do that.'

But Mahtab did worry. She lay still in the dark listening to her little sister's breathing. She tried to understand what her mother meant. Was it the guards with their torches? She had grown used to that. It happened at the same time every night, the boots, the turning of the door handle, the light flicking from Mum's face to hers, Soraya's and Farhad's. Sometimes she didn't even wake. Or was it someone else, someone who might mean harm to them? And in what way?

The nightmares began that night. She was on a mountain in a village that she didn't know and she was alone but she could see a small child, a girl on the other side of the road calling for her. Whenever Mahtab tried to cross the road, the child moved beyond her reach, still calling and calling her, begging Mahtab to reach her. The child had a face that Mahtab didn't recognise but she knew it was Soraya. Then the child had gone and Mahtab was running as if she was escaping from someone, but when she turned to see who was following her, there was no one. Still she ran. She knew she had to, even when her feet were cut and bloody. She ran so fast that she could not breathe. She called out for her mother or her father but no one came, and she was falling, falling.

She woke then.

The dream came every night. Sometimes it was Soraya who called her. Sometimes it was a boy with the face of a stranger, but she knew it was Farhad. Sometimes they were in the streets of Herat, sometimes in villages she didn't recognise. Always she ended up running and falling and always she woke before she landed.

Sometimes when she opened her eyes she found her mother kneeling on the floor, her face close, whispering soft words of consolation. 'It's all right, my little one, it's all right. You are safe now. Mumma's here. It's just a bad dream.'

Then Mahtab would say that it was nothing, she was fine, her mother should go back to bed, and she would roll over and push her face into the hard pillow and sleep again. One night, by chance, she felt in her pocket and her fingers closed over the tiny shell from the sand the night they took the boat. She rubbed the rough edges as she had that night, and remembered salt air filling her lungs, and the shimmering, beckoning water.

~~~

She slept later and later.

In the first few weeks, they had all got up and joined the breakfast queue soon after the meal began. As time went on, they were moved into the open camp and there they became part of the later meal group, the stragglers, and there were times when Mahtab told her mother that she wasn't hungry, that she didn't want to eat and she wasn't coming to the dining room. At first, her mother thought she was ill and let her stay in bed. She brought back bread from the kitchen, thin slices of soft white bread that Mahtab couldn't eat. After a few days of this, when Mahtab refused to see Catherine, her mother insisted that she get up when the others did, that she come to the dining room with them to eat.

'You must set an example to the others,' said her mother. 'If you give up, then how can I keep Farhad and Soraya well and happy?'

'How can anyone be well and happy here?'

'We must try, Mahtab. We must try.'

'Why? Why should we try? They do not want us here. Our father is gone. He should never have left us because now he's dead. You keep pretending, keep hoping. We have no hope, no life here.'

Her mother slapped her hard across the face. 'Do not say those words.'

Mahtab fell back against the bed, her cheek burning.

'Why not? You must think so too.'

'I do not know what to think. I just know who I am and that I am to look after you all and protect you.'

Mahtab dropped to the floor and drew her knees to her chest. She wrapped her arms around them and hid her face, rocking, silent.

～～

Mahtab watched her little brother and sister. Farhad still spent most days with Ahmad and Hussein, but their wild, joyful games grew fewer and fewer. One day they fought, wrestling in the dust, pushing and shoving, each grabbing the others by the hips, the shoulders, the neck, rolling over and over while other, bigger boys cheered them on. A guard, the woman who had shown them to the room the first day, laughed too. She threw her head back and the sun gleamed off her bright red lips and the flashes of gold in her teeth. The pink-and-ginger guard came then and spoke angrily to Hamida and to Mahtab's mother. He brought with him the translator, who said that they must control their sons or the boys would be put in special rooms by themselves where those who broke the rules were sent.

They had heard of these rooms. The prison within the prison. One of the Iraqi men from the boat, the one who had struck his wife, was there. He had attacked a guard, cursing him and his country, using language that Mahtab's father had once said belonged only with sailors and common criminals. For ten days he was alone there while his wife and his children begged the guards to let him out.

'They wouldn't do that to a child, would they?' Mahtab's mother wept as she spoke to the translator. He just rolled his eyes. 'It's a warning,' he said. 'Tell them.'

So the boys were made to listen as their mothers told them in great detail of the risks they were taking.

'You will be alone with no one to talk to or to play with,' said Hamida. 'They will feed you only bread and water – the bread they have here which you don't like. You must be friends. You must support each other. We will not be here for ever.'

After that, Hamida and Mahtab's mother made sure that every day one of them was watching. If it seemed a fight was coming between the boys they broke them apart. When they felt that older boys, bored in the long, hot day, goaded the younger ones to brawl they spoke harshly to them and brought Farhad and Ahmad inside. Sometimes they felt nervous when they saw the older men watching their boys.

'They are just missing their own children,' said Hamida. 'Our husbands would be the same.'

'Maybe. But I trust no one,' said Mahtab's mother and she watched all the more closely.

Chapter Eleven

ONE LUNCHTIME THEY were sitting in the dining room, stirring their rice and vegetables, talking of nothing in particular, when they heard loud screaming. A woman burst into the room, shouting and crying. Other women jumped up and ran to her and the guard grabbed her hand and called for a translator. The woman didn't wait but pulled the guard with her back through the door and in the direction of the shower block. Mahtab joined the crowd that gathered near the door. Two of the Iraqi women came out, carrying a girl. She was the one they had seen the first day, the girl who walked the wire. Her wet scarf hung almost to the ground. Her eyes were closed, her face a sickly grey.

'She drank the shampoo,' whispered one of the women.

'The whole bottle?'

'Why?'

'Crazy.'

'This place is enough to do that.'

'We will all end up like her.'

Mahtab watched as the girl was carried away towards the sickroom. She turned, thinking of shampoo creeping into her closed eyes, stinging, spitting out the tiny drops that got in her mouth. How could she? A whole bottle. She walked back to their room, her lunch forgotten.

~~~~~

Now there were days when English lessons weren't enough, days when Mahtab stretched on her bed and could not be drawn from it.

'Come on,' said her mother one afternoon. 'I've found the chess set, the one we made in Pakistan.'

Pakistan. Was it only months away? Mahtab felt she had lived in this centre for ever.

'Come on,' Farhad joined in. 'I want to play. Mum says you have to play with me.'

'Go away. Play by yourself. Play with Ahmad.'

'He doesn't know how.'

'Teach him.'

'Come on,' Soraya climbed on the bed beside her

sister. 'Show me what to do. I've forgotten. Tell me where the queens and the castles and the pawns go.'

Mahtab rolled over and pushed herself from the bed. Her body was a dead weight: an anchor resting on the bottom, needing some other stronger person to lift it. She shook her head, trying to focus.

'Are you all right?' said her mother from the doorway. 'I'll get Catherine.'

'No. I just need a minute.' She took deep breaths and pushed the air from her lungs with as much force as she could muster. 'Where are we playing?'

~~~

The next day, after breakfast, Mahtab sat on the step. Soraya had gone with their mother to help Hamida with the baby. Farhad was there too with Ahmad. She stared at the fence that was about fifty metres away. When she let her eyes go out of focus, the wire mesh faded and she found herself concentrating on the red dust beyond it. A breeze had started and it whipped the dust into a circle. At first it stayed low and then it turned into a tube that rose higher and higher, gathering more and more dust into it, dancing, teasing, blowing quickly every which way before her eyes. The dark redness of it grew paler as it moved upwards until the top disappeared, floating into the air. She stood up and ran to the fence. She gripped it, twisting her fingers through the spaces between the wire joins. Then she let go and moved along, trailing her fingers, her eyes still on the dust swirling, leaping, flying free in the hot morning air.

Gradually, it died. She stayed there, not moving. Would it return? It would. It must. She stared out at the wide, red land. *Come on, wind.* She moved along the fence a little. Maybe it would start up in another place. She walked further and further. The air was still. She heard but took no notice of the voices in the yard behind her: the quarrelling children, the softer talk of men with each other, of the women. She saw only the land: the broad, flat, treeless hugeness of it. She reached the place where a building blocked her way. She could go no further. What if the dancing wind had come again, behind her back? She turned and walked the way she had come, staring, still staring.

Some time later, her mother found her there. 'What are you doing?'

'Nothing.'

'Don't be silly. Come back to our room.'

'No.'

'Come and talk to me.'

'No.'

'We could do some English.'

'No.'

'What are you looking at?'

'Out there.'

'There's nothing out there.'

Mahtab didn't answer. She pulled her veil across her face and followed her mother to their room.

~~~

The next day she went again to the wire. She pressed herself against it, searching the land beyond it for anything that moved: for dust, for a bird, for a wavering blade of grass. Nothing. She began her walk. Step by step she counted her way, 'One, two, three, four...' She counted the words out loud: 'Five, six, seven...' At one hundred and fifty she reached the building and turned around. One hundred and fifty brought her back again and this time she went further. Two hundred steps took her to the place where another fence cut across the one she was travelling along. She turned again. She looked up and saw high above her a black speck against the blue of the sky. Two specks. Black birds hovering, their wings spread wide. The land below was still. She kept walking, counting, walking, counting, walking.

~~~

Late that afternoon, Catherine came to their room.

'Are you all right, Mahtab?'

'Yes.'

'I saw you walking today. Do you want to tell me why you do that?'

Mahtab didn't answer. It was a stupid question. Why did anyone walk? You walked to get where you wanted to go.

'Your mum is worried about you.'

Still no answer.

'You know you can come and talk to me if you want to. I'm not a guard here. I'm the nurse. I'm your friend.'

Friend. Mahtab let out a long, slow breath. Leila was her friend. Her only friend. Together, days after Aunt Mina's wedding, they had painted their feet with henna and danced for Grandma, who had clapped and fed them sweet sugared almonds from Paris.

'You do know that, don't you?' Catherine stood up and moved to the door. 'You can trust me.'

Mahtab stared at the tiny jar on the shelf. A shaft of sunlight came through the window and bounced off the earth inside it. The flecks of quartz gleamed shiny, silver. She was still staring at it when she heard Catherine quietly close the door.

The next day she walked again. And the next. She saw a coach approaching, racing towards them on the hot, dark bitumen. She did not turn to see it enter the camp and spill its load of new arrivals.

Days later as she stood in the hot midday sun, her head began to ache. She pushed it so hard against the wire that when she lifted it, she could feel the pattern of the strands was pressed into the skin of her forehead. Her mouth was dry. Strange flashes of light appeared at the corners of her eyes. She stumbled across the yard. 'Mum,' she called. 'Mum.'

Hamida caught her as she reached the steps.

'Mahtab, what's the matter?'

'Mum.'

'She's at the laundry. Let me.' She led Mahtab to her room and helped her onto the bed. She brought a mug of water. The flashes were still there, behind the closed lids.

Then her mother was there, putting her cool, wet hands on Mahtab's forehead. 'You're so hot. No more getting out in that sun for you.' She wet a corner of a towel and sponged Mahtab's face. 'Try to sleep. I'll stay near.'

All through the afternoon, she kept replacing the cool towel. When Soraya and Farhad came noisily into the room, she shooed them out. 'Go and play with the baby. Mahtab's not well.'

Mahtab missed dinner. That night she slept fitfully. She found the shell that she had placed under her pillow. Her hand closed over it and would not let it go. Then dreams began, but just as the images formed in her mind, she woke to find her mother watching over her. When morning came she was still hot.

151

'I think we should get Catherine,' said her mother.

'No. It's just the sun. That's what you said.'

All morning she tossed on the bed. Sweat gathered in the creases of her neck, her elbows and behind her knees. Her hair was wet and tangled. She was hot and sticky.

Some time in the afternoon Catherine did come. She sat beside Mahtab on the bed and took her hand. She ruffled Mahtab's hair. 'I'll call in and check on you. You'll be right as rain by the end of the week.'

Mahtab heard her through a strange mist. One moment she felt heavy, her body pressing into the mattress as if dragged down with heavy stones. Then she was floating, weightless above the bed, looking down on herself as she lay before her anxious mother.

Her head ached. She was so hot she wanted to throw the blanket from her, then she felt as frozen as she had been in the snow country. No blankets in the world could make her warm again.

For days she lay like that. Barely realising it, she allowed her mouth to be opened to take sips of water or spoonfuls of mashed-up food. Her mother and Catherine gently bathed her. All day, Soraya or Farhad stood beside her bed fanning her with the dampened towel. She wanted to reach out and speak to everyone but before she could form the words they had slipped from her brain and she could not call them back.

On the third night she seemed hotter and more restless.

The dreams came again, but like nothing she had dreamt before. They began with the child who was calling, who was Soraya but not Soraya, the face was different. She disappeared and there was a mountain and Mahtab knew she had to climb that mountain even though there was snow and she had no shoes and her feet were cut and bleeding. She could hear the voice again and she cried out I am coming, I am coming but no sound came from her voice and she knew she had to turn up the volume but her switch was broken and she couldn't find it then she was gathering dirt and stones for her mother, to remember the place by, every stone she saw she had to put it in her pocket but her pockets were full and the stones were heavy and still the voice was crying to her as she was bent beneath the weight of the stones, their sparkling silver quartz was making her eyes water so she took off her veil and wrapped them but she knew the black turbans were somewhere near and so she tossed the stones aside and she was in a truck riding in the front and it was her grandfather who was driving and he turned and said to her we are nearly there now, nearly there, and he was gone and it was her mother who was driving but she had a face that Mahtab didn't know and she was singing the La La song and she said sing with me, sing with me and Mahtab opened her mouth but no words come out which was strange because she was making the words in her head. Her father was driving now, driving through the red dust, and the truck was leaving the ground behind and it was rising higher and higher like the red dust and outside the window there were people waving, Leila and Hamida and then the baby and it was saying something but Mahtab couldn't hear her.

Later, or maybe it was the same dream, the same night, she was on a boat and her mother was there and she was saying something about her father that he is a good, good man, no he was a good, good man for he is dead and Mahtab tried to scream no, no he cannot be but again no sound came and then she was gone and Mahtab was alone and she knew that Farhad was somewhere and she had to find him but the rain had come and snow too and she was running on the boat and there was an earthquake, for the boat was rocking, rocking and it began to go up so maybe it was an aeroplane but it was just a whale, a lovely whale, and she wanted to lie down and stroke its head but she was Sinbad and she was falling, falling, falling.

~~~~

Her eyes opened. The dark room was lit by a candle. Catherine and her mother were there watching her.

'Farhad and Soraya, where are they, where?'

'Sshh. Everything's all right. They are with Hamida. You have been very ill.' Her mother patted her forehead.

Catherine was crying. 'I am so sorry, Mahtab. So sorry. You have been so sick. I had nothing to give you.'

'Dad? Is Dad...? You told me...' Mahtab reached for her mother.

'I haven't told you anything. You've been dreaming. What did you dream I said?'

'That he is dead. That he...'

'Nothing has changed, Mahtab. You've been gone from us for a few days. Your fever has been so strong. That is all. We still don't know.'

Mahtab lay back. She opened her clutched hand. The tiny shell fell from her outstretched fingers.

Chapter Twelve

THE NEXT DAY Mahtab sat up. Her mother knelt behind her, brushing her hair and then plaiting it and winding it up off her neck. Every now and then she leant forward and wrapped her arms around her daughter. 'I was so scared,' she said. 'So scared that you were really, really sick and you were going to leave us.'

'You mean die?'

'Mmm.'

'I thought so too, Mum.' She was quiet for a moment. Then she said, 'Mum, you know how I said one day that Dad was dead. Do you think he is? Do you think they'll send us back?'

'Only in my worst, my darkest thoughts. And then sometimes I am certain that he is alive. He is out there, somewhere in this country, and he is thinking something has happened to us. Maybe he is locked up too. Maybe he is in a city and he has telephoned Pakistan and they have told him we set out for Australia. He will be worried too, not knowing where we are. Some boats have sunk, you know. Catherine told me.'

'What can we do, Mum? What can we do?'

Her mother held her tightly. 'We wait. We wait and we get you well and then we stay strong and we believe that he will come. He has to come. He will come.' She started to rock then, slowly, rhythmically, humming the La La song for a very long time.

~~~

Two days later, Mahtab got out of bed for a while. She sat on the step in the sun and watched the yard, her face sheltered behind her veil. Catherine came to join her, squatting in the dust at her feet.

'How are you feeling?'

'A bit better.'

'You gave everyone a fright, you know.'

'So Mum tells me.'

'You Afghani girls must be made of very tough stuff.'

Mahtab laughed.

'That is the first time I've heard you laugh,' said Catherine. 'I'm going into town for the weekend. Can I get you anything?'

'Are you allowed to do that? Really?'

Catherine shrugged. 'I do what I do.'

'I'd ... I'd like a book,' said Mahtab.

'A book to read?'

'No. To write in.'

'You mean a diary.'

'I suppose.' A book to write in, every day. As Dad had said. If he came or if he didn't come, she would write down and remember.

'OK,' said Catherine, rising to her feet and brushing the dust from her jeans. 'I'll see what I can do.'

All weekend, Mahtab waited. She played a game of chess with Farhad, surprised to find that he had developed skills and tactics beyond those she had herself. She told the story of the kangaroo to Soraya twice and she watched Hamida's baby as she kicked and gurgled in the morning sun. She had a name now, Arezo, and Hamida said, 'One day, when we are all together with her father, and with yours, we will celebrate this new name properly with sweets and chocolate.'

Mahtab blew kisses on the little one's belly and stroked her arms, delighted at her skin as soft as velvet.

~~~

Catherine returned. 'I couldn't find a diary,' she said, 'it's too late in the year. So I brought you this.' She handed Mahtab an exercise book. 'You can put in the date yourself.'

It was a thick book, with a white spiral spine. Mahtab flicked through the lined pages and turned it over. On the back were tables of measurement: weights and distances in different systems and a yellow map of Australia. She knew it from the book her father had shown her.

'Can you point to where we are?'

Catherine held out a pen. 'I brought you this as well.' She took the book and marked a spot almost in the middle of the map.

'So far from anywhere,' whispered Mahtab.

When Catherine had gone, she turned to the clean first page.

~~~~

Day One

Dad, you told me long ago that I should write a diary, that I should write down everything that happens and then I could tell my grandchildren. I'm not sure about the grandchildren but this is really for you. I am not really sure about you either. Sometimes when it's dark at night and the others are sleeping I am all alone and I fear that you are dead, but I pray to Allah that you are alive and we will be together again. When it is so, I will read you bits of what I write down here, the way you read to us before.

You will not recognise me. I am almost as tall as Mum but I am skinny too, as I was not well for a while and I didn't eat. My trousers are creeping up almost halfway to my knee. I need Grandma to show me how to make some new ones — except I have no material.

It's too late to write things that have happened although I will tell you about them. At the moment I am not thinking of them, they are too full of thoughts I never want again. I am going to number the days till we meet.

It's hot here, always hot. We've had months of heat although the nights are growing colder now. Farhad and Soraya are playing cards. I have given Mum some pages from my book and she has drawn pictures for them and they are playing that game where you put the cards down and when yours is the same as the other ones you can claim the whole pile. I think Soraya is winning. She is taller too. They both are. We wonder if you still have a beard.

~~~~

The next morning, after breakfast, Hamida came into their room.

'Can you take Arezo for a while and watch Ahmad? I have been summoned to a meeting.'

Mum sat the baby on her hip. 'Do you think it's the visa? Will it have come?'

The other woman shrugged. 'Pray for me.' She straightened her scarf, tucked loose strands of hair behind her ears and headed for the administration building.

Mahtab and Soraya took the baby from Mum and put her on the bed. They tickled her till she chortled gleefully then squealed and clapped her tiny hands. Then Mahtab held her on her knee while Soraya danced. Soraya held her arms up and clicked her fingers and swayed and twirled around and the baby reached out for her, laughing again. They all laughed too.

They were still playing when Hamida came running back across the yard.

'I have it! I have it!' she cried as she came into the room. 'I wanted to dance and scream my way here but I couldn't in front of everyone else who is waiting.' Her smile fell away. 'I should not be so happy in front of you who don't yet know.'

'Don't be silly.' Mum put her arms around Hamida and kissed her. 'Be happy. It is a wonderful day. Our day will come.'

Word passed quickly through the centre. People knocked on the door and came in to congratulate Hamida, to help her pack her bags, to give her the names of their friends or relations in cities away in the south. She was hugged and kissed and Arezo was passed from hand to hand and more kisses were planted on the top of her head.

'Are we leaving?' asked Ahmad.

'We are going to meet your father.' Hamida knelt down and took his hands in hers.

'Can Farhad come with us?' Ahmad pushed her away and put his arm around Farhad.

His mother shook her head. 'Farhad must stay with his mum and sisters, just as you must come with us.'

'But if Farhad can't come, I don't want to go.' Tears filled Ahmad's eyes.

'He will follow soon. We can go first and find a place where they can come and join us.'

The boys ran back down the steps and into the yard.

'May it be so,' said Mahtab's mother. 'May it be so.'

~~~

Hamida spoke then of how the lawyers had found her husband. He was in Sydney and he'd been looking for her ever since he'd heard that she had left Afghanistan to follow him. In three days time she would join him. She could not believe her good fortune. He would meet his daughter for the first time. Arezo slept on her mother's chest, her thumb firmly in her mouth.

Within the hour, they were gone.

Mahtab took her diary and went out onto the step, under the light.

~~~

Day Two

Hamida has left for Sydney. She was smiling in a way we have never seen before. We are all so happy for her, it is wonderful news, but there is also a heavy stone in my heart that only our own visa can lift. How wonderful it would have been to go with them. Soon. Please soon.

~~~

'Do you think one day it will be us?' Soraya came and sat with Mahtab on the step.

'It will.'

'And will we learn the English that Catherine speaks with you?'

Mahtab nodded. 'You know lots of words already. When you get to school, it will come quickly. Catherine says that when you are very young, you learn best. You will learn more quickly than me or Farhad or Mum.'

'Maybe our dad speaks English now and he will have forgotten our language. Maybe he will have shaved off his beard and he will wear the shorts like these guards and he will be like an Australian man. He will be so different.'

163

'He will still be our dad,' said Mahtab. How similar Soraya's thoughts were to her own. Her worst fears: *He is dead and he will never come.* Fears that he was alive but somehow he had changed or they had changed and everything she wanted, had wanted now for so long, would not happen or would happen in a way that was not how she imagined it at all. Then there were times when she tried to remember, tried to imagine Afghanistan. It seemed to her that it was in a strange cloud, the buildings would not take a proper shape, her own house seemed like a toy house, floating in her mind, the people shrouded in veils of fine gauze such that they did not truly exist. No past. No future. Just this present. This unbearable now.

Chapter Thirteen

Day Three

Dad, Soraya wants to know if you still have a beard. Do you still look like our father?

It's hot, Dad, really hot. Did you know I was really, really sick? Silly to ask you that, of course you cannot know. Mum thought I was going to die, although she says she knew I wouldn't. I'm a lot better now. Mum is hoping for another interview soon. She's heard there are some new lawyers coming.

When Hamida left yesterday, she was with her lawyer in a big car. We all stood and waved until all we were waving at was the red dust. We are missing her and Ahmad and the baby. Farhad especially. He and Ahmad are like brothers. Arezo, that's the baby (she was born in Indonesia, just before we got on the boat), was sitting up and making noises as if she was trying to talk. At least that is what Hamida said, but we couldn't understand what she was saying. She was always ready to be played with when everything else was so boring.

Hamida's husband is in Sydney. That's where Mum hopes you are. Maybe Hamida's husband will be able to find you.

Mahtab put her pen down. A coach was coming through the gate. It pulled up in the centre of the yard and the ritual of assigning rooms began. There were no women and children this time, only men. They looked like Iraqis and Afghanis, some like her father. There was something strange about them: no appearance of fear, confusion or apprehension. They were not taken to the closed camp but came straight away to the main yard. They slung their bags over their shoulders and looked around. It was as if they had been through the whole process before.

~~~

The next morning, when Mahtab called to Farhad and Soraya that their mother wanted them in their room, one of the new arrivals looked up from the group where he was sitting. His eyes followed the children as they crossed the yard. Mahtab frowned.

~~~

'He's a strange one, Mum,' she whispered when she pointed him out in the dining room. 'He looks at us in a funny way. And he's coming over here.'

The tall stranger bowed to Mahtab's mother.

'I don't mean to alarm you, but are you the wife and daughter of Hussein Ahmady?'

'Hussein Ahmady? Ye-es.'

Her father. He knew their father. She grabbed her mother's arm.

'You know him? Where is he? Where? Is he all right?' Her mother was on her feet, seizing the stranger's hand, looking up at him, wide-eyed, waiting.

'He is in Sydney.'

'In Sydney.' One hand covered her mouth. Tears filled her eyes.

'He is my friend. We were together in another camp.'

'How is he? Is he well?' Her voice was strangely soft.

'He has his visa. He has moved a number of times. He will be so pleased to know you are safe. He was so worried last time I spoke to him.'

'You spoke to him?' The tears now ran down her cheeks.

'Of course. Many times. On the phone.'

'In Sydney.' Mahtab's mother slumped back in her chair. 'Thank God. Thank God.'

The man nodded and pulled up a chair beside her. 'I am so glad to bring you this news.'

She put her hand out to him. 'I don't know your name.'

'Moustafa.'

'Moustafa, you bring hope to me and my children. This is the best thing I have heard in more than a year. Do you know how to get in touch with him? Do you have his address? Can we write to him?'

Moustafa pulled a torn scrap of paper from his pocket and passed it across the table.

'Better than that, why don't you telephone him.'

~~~~

Tears and smiles, laughing and crying. One after the other and at the same time.

Mahtab's mother's hand was shaking so much that Moustafa had to dial the number and when the phone was answered he passed it to her without speaking.

Mahtab could hardly wait her turn. Surely now interviews would come. Visas would come. She took the receiver.

'Dad?'

'Mahtab. How are you?'

She couldn't answer. Tears streamed down her face. She gulped, swallowed salt. 'I'm...I'm all right. I'm well. I'm so happy we have found you.'

'Me too, my Mahtab. Me too.'

168

Farhad and Soraya each spoke and laughed and had long, empty silences and then the phone went back to her mother and calmer, practical talk began. Visas. Interviews. Lawyers. Mahtab, Soraya and Farhad drifted from the room. They sat on the step of their building. Words poured from them like water from a jar.

'He says he is the happiest man in the world to hear me speak.'

'And me.'

'He says he has his beard still.'

'He says he is going to a class to learn English.'

'He says he has many Afghani friends.'

'He says I can have a kite, he will have one for me when we meet.'

'He wants to come and get us but it is not possible.'

'He says he is in a city as far away from us as from Herat to Kabul twenty times.'

'He says he is sure that we will be with him soon.'

We will be with him soon.

~~~

Day Five

Dad, that phone call was so good. We are all so happy now and we cannot wait to speak to you again. Next week I think. I want to ask you if there is a school

near where you live and will I go there and are there
neighbours with a girl my age. I cannot believe that our
time here may be over. I thought I would be here for ever.
Mum says that she will apply for another meeting in the
morning and that we must not get too excited because it
may be some time before they will speak with her. I cannot
believe they will keep us here when they know that you,
our father, are waiting. I am happy, happy, happy.

~~~

When their mother went for her next meeting, Mahtab, Farhad and Soraya sat on the bed and waited. 'We should do some English,' Mahtab said, but her mind was with her mother and Catherine's book stayed unopened. Could they say no? Could they find a reason to reject them?

'When are we going to Dad?' said Soraya.

'I don't know. Soon I hope.'

'How long is soon?'

'I don't know.'

~~~

Weeks passed.

'They need more proof of who we are,' said their mother when she returned. 'They need to check that we have been truthful, that I am your mother, that I am your father's wife, that we did leave our country for the reasons we have said. We have lawyers who will speak for us.'

'But we have told the truth. We are who we say we are.'

'I know. You know. The lawyers know. It is not enough. We must wait longer. It will not be for ever.'

These days now were the hardest of all.

Sometimes Mahtab lay on the bed, staring at the ceiling, in a strange, still, non-existence. Sometimes she sat on the step watching the ants that crossed the yard in long, narrow lines, or her eye was taken by a skinny lizard, sunning itself on a rock. She stared across at the wire and the red dust beyond. Had she been a different person then? In the afternoons she took up the books Catherine had given her and studied, committing words and phrases to memory as if her life depended on it.

How are you? I am very well, thank you. And you? I am Mahtab from Afghanistan. I am twelve years old and I have a younger brother and a younger sister. I like reading and writing and I am very happy to be here. I like tea but I do not like to drink coffee.

And then there were times when she wrote in her diary.

~~~

Day Fifteen
Not all these pages are for other people to read. I do not want anyone to know that I am scared. Scared of who I must be to live in this new country. Scared I have to

change the way I look and think and feel. I don't want to change. At least, I don't think I want to. I want to wake up in my own bed, in my own old room and find Grandma is making the tea in the morning and there is the smell of bread. And Farhad and Reza are playing the way they did before. And then I think of Grandpa, and I know nothing is the same there and I cannot be there, maybe ever. And then I think it is not right that I should never see that place again. How dare someone stop me from being with that part of my family! Maybe when I am older things will change and we will be able to go back. Till then I am stuck here just thinking and then I think that I think too much and I know how it is that people go crazy.

~~~

Moustafa came every day. He sat in the sun and told them of when he was in the camp with their father. 'He talked about you all the time. One day you must meet my children, he said. They are the best kids, the smartest kids in the world. Mahtab, Farhad, Soraya – he missed you so much.' He ruffled Farhad's hair. 'I got sick of hearing about you. Especially you.'

'What did he say about me?' asked Soraya.

'Ahh.' Moustafa rubbed his chin. 'He said you were a chatterbox. You loved to sing and to splash around in a wading pool in the back yard.'

She sat back then, satisfied.

'Have you got any kids?' asked Mahtab.

He shook his head. 'No. I never married – well, not yet, anyway.'

'Then you could be our uncle,' said Farhad. 'Our other uncles are too far away now, so we can have you instead.'

'Thank you.' Moustafa turned his face away as he spoke. 'Thank you.'

~~~

Other times he spoke of why he was there, with them in this camp. He told how in the other place the men had been in despair. One had climbed onto the roof and thrown himself at the wire. Others had sewn their lips together in silent protest. Still others had lit fires and burned buildings and so they had been separated, placed on coaches and driven to other centres around the country.

~~~

There were more phone calls. Each week they joined the group that gathered on the verandah near the kitchen and waited their turn. Sometimes there were tears. Sometimes joking and laughter. Other times it felt as if their father had gone away for a few days and was simply checking how they were before his return. Their mother went to meetings with the men in the administration building. She was joined there by lawyers, who came in their shiny cars, carrying briefcases and mopping the sweat from their foreheads with white handkerchiefs.

After each meeting she returned to the room, saying only, 'It won't be long now.'

~~~~

Day Thirty-four
It is true. We are accepted. We have the visa.
We are coming to you, Dad. We are coming.

~~~~

Late in the morning an officer strode across the yard and up the steps and banged on the door. He handed over documents. 'Your visas,' he said. 'There'll be a car in an hour.'

An hour.

Frantic packing. Quick showering. Snatched conversations with those who came to congratulate, to hug and wish the very best to them all. Mahtab's small bag bulged and parts of the stitching gave way to reveal the socks and gloves, unworn since Pakistan. They stood in the doorway, looking back to check that nothing had been left behind.

'The jar. Where is the jar?'

'Don't worry, Mum, I put it in my bag.' Mahtab patted the outside pocket where the tiny jar rested against her shell from Indonesia. There would be an Australian shelf to hold them both.

~~~~

Day Thirty-five

We are in Adelaide. We came in on the coach last night.
It was late in the afternoon when we joined the main road
and there was a huge tree by itself and the leaves seemed like
they were yellow as well as green and as we drove past they
all took off into the air. They were birds, Dad, tiny green
and yellow birds. So beautiful and Soraya and I laughed
and I don't know when I last felt so happy.

It is strange how in one way I felt sad when we left
the Centre. In another way of course I wanted to shout and
cheer and bang drums in celebration. The boy Hussein's
family cried when they waved us goodbye. Two other
families from Afghanistan were with us and some men from
Africa too. This evening we are taking the train but I think
the others will stay here. There are people who will look
after them. These people met our coach and brought us food
and asked us if we wanted anything. They were so kind but
what I really wanted was to say we have need of nothing
but our father. In such a few short days we will be with
you. After all this time I cannot believe it.

~~~

Day Thirty-six

Melbourne. Mum teased us today. She said we could get
a hotel and we could stay the night and we could be like
visitors to the city and look at everything there is here, even
a zoo. Soraya was almost tempted because she so wants
to see her first kangaroo but I could not believe that Mum

175

would delay meeting with you for one second more than we must. Then she laughed and we knew she was joking. We take the train this afternoon and we will travel all night to you.

Will you be waiting for us on the platform?
Will you?

Chapter Fourteen

MAHTAB CANNOT SIT still. Up and down the aisle she walks, peering out at hour after hour of cows, sheep, cars and gum trees. There are small towns too. The train doesn't stop at them, just at a larger one, but she doesn't climb down.

'I don't know how long it will wait here,' says her mother, her back pressed into the corner of her seat, Soraya asleep on her lap.

The train starts again. How can Soraya sleep? Mahtab thinks of counting the sheep, counting forwards, not backwards. Always counting. Will it make the time go more quickly? There are more farms. More small towns. More cows and sheep. And there are hills with soft yellow grasses and mountains – small ones but mountains nevertheless. This country is not all flat and reddish-brown.

Finally there are suburbs. Kilometre after kilometre, brick houses set back in rich green gardens with low fences, open to the street. Then neat brick stations, with signs, but the train moves so quickly that she cannot read their names. The train doesn't stop at them.

Mahtab checks herself in the mirror. She brushes a stray strand of hair that has escaped her veil. She looks down at her hands, her scratched fingers, her chipped and broken nails. Will they recognise him? Will he have changed too? Will he know them? What is Mum feeling? She looks across at her mother. *Her eyes are closed. Is she dreaming of him? Is she searching her mind for pictures of him, as I am? Can she see him that night he left us in Pakistan, the way he was before that, at home, by the table, warming his feet on the brazier, laughing and telling us stories as he took the bread and dipped it in the bowl?*

Outside, the houses are closer together, older-looking with red roofs. Above them birds are flying, white against the deep, deep blue sky. The train is slowing. There are other trains now, heading in the opposite direction. The houses are further back from the tracks. Strangers in the carriage are standing up,

straightening their clothes, taking down their luggage.
It is nearly time. It must be time.

Slowly, slowly the train draws in alongside a
platform. It stops. Mahtab looks beyond the signs and
machines. People move and pour out of the door.

Mahtab takes her bag.

Drops it.

Pushes past strangers.

Steps from the train.

Searches faces.

Sees him.

Runs to him.

Throws herself and is caught by his arms, his
beard, his breath, his voice, his tears, his loving,
loving tears.

Three weeks later

Mahtab stands on a grassy hill looking down at the sea. Her mother, her father, her brother and sister stand with her. She takes in the naked arms and legs, the bare backs, the midriffs, the bodies stretched out on the sand and playing around the edges of the water. She gazes at the waves crashing and the board riders dazzling as they twist and turn and point the noses of their boards to the shore.

And above her, the kites.

It's the Festival of the Winds. Kites from every nation are there. The sea breeze catches them and draws them higher and higher. Bold, bright red ones, long-tailed dangling ones, huge ones, baby ones for little children, rainbow kites, box kites, insect shapes, squares and triangles, they mix and dance together.

180

'Let's move along where there is more room,' says her father. They walk past the pavilion, breathing in the smoke of meat, cooking on a host of barbecues and the tang of salt air. Soraya has taken off her sandals. Clutching them she runs down the sand to the water, laughing as the waves tickle, and then she retreats, before racing back to the spot they have chosen on the grass.

Their father opens a bag he has been carrying. Two kites tumble onto the grass: one purple and red, and one deep blue. He takes them up and tests the plastic handles and the strings.

'No cutting strings,' he says, 'but good all the same.'

Farhad and Soraya run together, yelling, the kites trailing behind them. Down the grassy hill they go and the wind grabs the fabric and lifts the kites higher and higher.

They come back and fall down, laughing and gasping for breath.

'My turn.' Mahtab takes the red-and-purple kite. She wraps her fingers around the plastic handle. She has never done this before.

Slowly, she runs. The wind lifts the edges of her veil and the hem of her tunic. Faster and faster. Her father is smiling and her mother is clapping as the kite lifts and begins its drift upwards. Mahtab gazes up at it, mouth open, heart full. Happiness and joy. The kite is dancing, tugging against her, veering first left and then right. Caught by an eddy, it swirls round and then dives straight towards her. Mahtab holds her breath. She stands her ground. More wind comes. It takes the kite soaring again, higher and higher. The red-and-purple fabric is shimmering, triumphant against the cloudless sky.

181

About this story

Mahtab's Story began in a classroom at Holroyd High School in western Sydney in 2004. I was interested in writing about the experience of being a Muslim girl in Australia in the twenty-first century and the principal, Dorothy Hoddinott, had arranged for me to meet some students in Year 11. The group was made up of girls who were refugees from Iraq and Afghanistan. Their stories of persecution and fear in their own countries and of their escape to Australia were so compelling that I felt I had to write about that experience.

One girl, Nahid Karimi, expressed great interest in my work. She felt strongly that the story should be told of what she and others like her had been through. We became friends and she shared with me the details of her family's flight from Herat, the long period of waiting in Pakistan while her father went ahead and then the journey to Australia and the period of imprisonment in a detention centre.

Nahid has now left school and is a student at the University of Western Sydney.

Mahtab's Story is a novel, not a biography of Nahid. I have varied the events, added and subtracted to shape the story. Without her contribution, however, this book could not have been written. I am forever indebted to her and her family and I am in awe of their courage.

Libby Gleeson

You might also enjoy these books

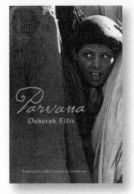

When soldiers burst into her home and drag her father off to prison, Parvana is forced to take responsibility for her whole family. *Parvana* is a story of courage in the face of overwhelming fear.

Parvana's Journey is the riveting story of a young girl's talent for friendship, hope and gritty determination despite the ravages of war.

Alone in a foreign city, away from the refugee camp, Shauzia must scrounge through rubbish to find food, huddle in doorways to sleep. But with the help of her dog Jasper she is determined to make her way in the world.

www.allenandunwin.com